Triad of Time

A Time Travel Novel

Triad of Time

A Time Travel Novel

K. F. Whatley

Published by KF Whatley
Zebulon, North Carolina USA

Triad of Time

A Time Travel Novel

Paperback ISBN: 978-1-7359260-3-2
e-book ISBN: 978-1-7359260-4-9
Large Print Paperback ISBN: 978-1-7359260-5-6

First Printing 2020 by KF Whatley

www.FictionWriterNC.com

In memory of Frank, and for all who miss him

Other works by this author

Making Corrections: A Time Travel Novel

Acknowledgements

I'm grateful to the editors, beta readers, and patient family and friends who supported me and made this sequel possible. Special thanks to Corvi, Cindy, Nadia, Juli, Cole, Riley, Kim B., and the Second Cup Writers' Group for their review and encouragement.

1 – Blink

Peter Braggin ran full speed down the slope. Behind him, his pursuer crashed through the brush, closing the gap between them. Peter knew his head start was fading fast.

He managed to keep his footing all the way down the hill, hopping the last few feet to reach the bottom with, he estimated, a fifty-yard lead. Furtively scanning the terrain, he spotted a pond off to his left. He raced toward it, stumbling several times before reaching the water.

Crouching low to conceal himself, he heard a thump and loud cursing as his pursuer fell and rolled to the bottom of the hill. He committed the deep, angry voice to his memory.

He scanned the water's edge and picked up the first item he spotted in the moonlight. It was a small length of dead reed; too soft to be a weapon, but it would serve his purpose. He wanted something to grip in his hand, an object on which to focus, to calm his mind for the return to his own time.

Peter took a few deep breaths and rolled quietly sideways into the pond. He sank to the murky bottom, letting the dark waters envelop him, and tightened his grip on the reed.

Above him, he felt his pursuer approaching the pond's edge. He knew waiting to see the man's face would be unwise; his position wasn't defensible. He must go.

Closing his eyes, the time traveler pictured his home years away and, before he ran out of breath, he disappeared from the pond.

***

Peter blinked awake on his bed. Staring at his bedroom ceiling, he drew in a long breath, letting the relief at being in his own place, his own time, rush through him. "That was close," he said aloud to the empty room.

His plan had been to get a look at the killer, and if possible, to save his victim. Instead, he'd been spotted before he could see anything; chased and nearly caught. Losing his element of surprise was unexpected. As a time traveler, he was used to getting the drop on people. Well, not this time.

His clothes were damp. He knew that he'd been in them for a while, although it felt like only seconds had passed since he'd been in the pond. Hands resting on his stomach, the bit of reed was firmly clasped in his left hand.

Rolling out of bed, he tossed the reed into a trash basket. That was one out-of-its-time item he wouldn't be storing for future use. He surveyed himself in the bathroom mirror, peeling a leaf from his chin and scratching the skin beneath its muddy outline. His water-darkened curls stuck to his forehead, and he ruffled them with his fingers. Another leaf dislodged, dropping onto the sink.

Undressing, he balled up his damp, swampy-smelling clothes, wrapped them in the muddied comforter from the bed, and carried them out to the laundry room before returning to the bathroom.

Showering thoroughly, he washed his hair three times until he stopped smelling the filthy pond water. After a quick towel-dry, he pulled on his boxers and blue jeans, and threw on a button-down shirt. Then, in bare feet, he took the stairs two-by-two down to his basement office.

Peter's first order of business: check the news and social media. As with all his trips through time, he confirmed his changes to the timeline, ensuring he hadn't broken anything big, even though he had already felt his slight change fall into place.

He absentmindedly buttoned his shirt as he scanned the headlines.

The only change he had managed was interrupting the killer, which had caused the man to move the body. According to the news articles from two days prior, her body had been found around the same time it had originally — early in the morning on a hot first of September — but now it had been found near Nashville, North Carolina. Before his trip back in time, it had been found closer to Spring Hope and the pond where he'd taken a dunk.

He found a few photographs posted on Twitter. None showed anything other than the terrain he'd seen last night, and the county responders.

Still in Nash County, he thought. That provided him with a bit of new information about the killer's potential comfort zone. He'd failed to make the correction he'd wanted, and, sadly, hadn't changed the fate of the killer's victim: a 20-year-old woman named Silvia Andrews. He chastised himself for not better preparing to save her. Yet, he knew more about the killer now, and he was going to count last night as a semi-successful trip in that regard. Plus, time was on his side, and he could try again.

Not for the first time, he wished his grandfather was still around. Two heads were better than one, and Peter doubted he'd have failed so badly if Grampa had been there to help. At that thought, he shook his head. *The old man and me, would we really have done much better for poor Silvia? But who else is there?*

When the time traveler finished reading the news reports, he headed for the kitchen to make his morning coffee and devise a better plan. He would try again. For Silvia's sake, he must.

***

On the tenth of September, Peter turned on the morning news and learned that another woman's body had been found. He kicked himself, having failed twice to save Silvia Andrews. Now another woman was dead, an equally young Valerie Edmonds.

Since deciding he needed help, he'd spent too many days thinking about where to find it. He'd come up with the answer last night, and it would take time to set that plan in motion; yet, now, a second woman was dead.

Yes, he had all the time in the world, in theory. With two women and their families suffering, though, he wanted to move faster. He chastised himself for letting his frustration from his failed attempts make him overly cautious.

The news program switched to a live shot, complete with uniformed officers trudging through a wooded area beside a road. "The body was reported by a farmer who found it while working in his nearby field. According to a source, the woman was nude, found with only a *very old* watch on the body, which one police source, who wishes to remain anonymous, tells me is believed to be a message to police — although it is not yet known what that message might be."

The on-scene reporter then poetically added that vultures had been circling the area over the crime scene. "Initial speculation," he said, "is that Valerie Edmonds' body may have been left on this quiet country road just hours before it was found. I've been told they expect to release more details later. Back to you, Bob."

Before moving on to the next story, the anchor mentioned the similarities with the body found nine days earlier, that of Silvia Andrews, age 20. Both had been discovered with an antique watch. The anchor, face grim, reminded viewers both bodies were found nude — his eyes twinkling a bit too much for Peter's taste. Then, the anchor asked viewers with information on the women or missing antique watches to contact the county sheriff's office, with the phone number displayed at the bottom of the screen. Seconds later, the anchor moved on to the next local news story. He turned the TV off.

That's two women now, Peter thought. *If I'm going to save them, I need help. No more delay. It's time to make the call.*

2 – Help

Carrie Weathers sat in her favorite spot on the couch, sipping her coffee and editing a draft news article on her laptop. It was the last day of September, and she was rushing to finish the article announcing an upcoming pumpkin festival.

She looked up as Mig joined her on the couch, leaning in for a kiss before settling into his seat.

Carrie looked her husband up and down, smiling. Miguel "Mig" Weathers was the epitome of tall, dark, and handsome. His salt-and-pepper hair complemented his golden skin. "Silver and gold," Carrie would playfully call him, prompting him to roll his eyes. Mig wore a well-maintained mustache, and sometimes a goatee — depending on how he felt when he shaved each morning.

Carrie, seven years younger and a foot shorter, adored Mig, who treated her as if she were perfect. She knew she was far from it, though she thought that *he* was as close to perfect as a human being could get.

The Weathers lived in eastern North Carolina, unaware they shared their town with a time traveler. Their modest home sat just beyond the Hope Wells town limits, surrounded by a mix of houses, trailers, and farms. Together, the husband and wife ran a news website, with Mig as photographer and advertising salesman, and Carrie as reporter and editor. While most of the news they covered dealt with local happenings, they prided themselves on reporting strange news: the crop circles, Bigfoot sightings, and UFOs prevalent in the state. Most recently, they'd joined a Bigfoot search team, covering the search and the sighting that preceded it.

Carrie leaned over to give Mig another kiss, lingering on his lips until his mustache tickled, then sat back, splashing her coffee on her shirt. "Good morning again," Mig said, grabbing a tissue and handing it to her.

She dabbed at her yet-another-mess — she accepted that she made more messes than the children ever had — as Mig flipped on the television and tuned to a local news channel. He grabbed his tablet computer, and settled back, drinking his coffee while he scanned the latest articles Carrie had published to their news site. The TV news played on as background noise, mostly ignored, as they bantered while they worked.

Mig and Carrie started each day with coffee and planning, interspersing discussions about customers and family. The morning was proceeding normally until Mig's cell phone rang. As Carrie reached for the television's mute button, he waived her off and stepped out of the room to answer. She heard Mig speaking to the caller for a few minutes, catching little of his side of the conversation over the voice of the news anchor.

Ending the call, Mig returned to the living room. "That was Peter Braggin," Mig said. "He's invited us over to his house for dinner tomorrow night." Mig's eyebrows were raised in a what-the-heck expression.

"Oh," Carrie said, puzzled, "Nothing for years and now he calls us twice within a month? That's a little odd. But then, he's an odd guy. What did you tell him?"

"I told him we'd come. Okay with you?"

"Sure," Carrie said. Of course, it was okay with her. She was always on the lookout for news stories, and Mr. Braggin had recently shared one of their weirdest. Carrie asked. "Does he want us to bring anything?"

Mig shook his head, "Nah. He said don't worry about it. He's got it covered. Tomorrow at 7 o'clock."

Carrie's brow furrowed. "Why do you think he's invited us for dinner? I can count on one hand — actually one finger —

the number of *dinner* invitations we've had from people we've interviewed. Lunch, maybe, but dinner is unusual. And at his house?"

"Yeah. He's different," Mig said, without expanding on it. He didn't need to say more. Carrie knew what he meant. Mr. Braggin was definitely different. The man looked to be almost the same age as Mig, fifty-ish. Both times they'd seen him, his hair had been unkempt, his social skills lacking. They'd nicknamed him Spiky Hair Guy. While he spoke fast and went off on many tangents, his words were almost mesmerizing. There was something about him that made people feel comfortable, at ease. "His comment did get me to the doctor, you know. Probably kept me from getting really sick."

"I know," Carrie said, a shiver running through her. On the day they'd met him, Mr. Braggin's suggestion to Mig that he didn't look well had led to Mig getting a physical, catching his cancer early, and was in large part responsible for his current state of recovery.

The Weathers had first met Peter Braggin, a self-proclaimed expert on the ethics of time travel, years earlier at a paranormal exposition. Mr. Braggin was a speaker, and held court at an expo booth. The Weathers had covered the event for their newspaper. Mig and Carrie had both found the man interesting back then, and were intrigued when he contacted them earlier in September. He'd re-introduced himself, inviting them to his home to write an article on a haunting. He had told them, then, that his house had been haunted for years, and been in his family for decades.

Mig had taken several convincing photographs on that recent visit, capturing a glowing "presence" in Mr. Braggin's office. A photo published alongside Carrie's article had become popular, with thousands of hits per day in its second week.

During that visit, the three of them had discussed his "ghost" along with memories of his expo presentation. Mig had taken the opportunity to thank Mr. Braggin for the part he played in Mig beating cancer. After the somber moment passed, the two men had joked and talked for a long while, as Carrie had mostly listened, enthralled.

That visit had been mid-September. It was the first of October now, as they drove to his house for dinner.

"Maybe he just wants to talk about his haunting more," Carrie speculated.

"Maybe. You know, I like the guy. Strange but interesting. Like the news we cover," Mig snarked. He and Carrie chuckled in tandem.

"Well, if he wants to talk about his ghost again, it's good timing. I can write a follow-up article for Halloween. It'll be here before we know it."

Carrie pointed. "There's his house number, on the black mailbox coming up. Wow, big place!"

Turning the steering wheel, Mig pulled the car onto Mr. Braggin's driveway and parked, shutting off the engine. He mused, "I'm gonna enjoy talking with him again. He's got interesting views."

That makes two of you, Carrie thought. She was looking forward to hearing their discussions. Mig got along with almost everyone, but he and Peter Braggin had fallen into easy, in-depth conversation, even friendly debates, during their mid-September visit.

Exiting the car, Mig walked around it and met Carrie as she emerged. He took her hand in his, and together they walked up the sidewalk to Peter Braggin's front door, Mig commenting on the neat and tidy edging along the walk.

Carrie laughed, "Yeah, he must be like you and serious about taking care of his yard."

***

Peter Braggin ushered the Weathers into his expansive dining room and motioned for each of them to sit, pointing Carrie to a chair to his right, and Mig to a seat opposite her. Peter then took his seat at the head of the ornate, antique table — one built to seat many more than three, Carrie noted. She also noted he was well-groomed this time, his usually erratic hair slicked down, and his button-down shirt and tan pants neatly pressed.

On the table sat a bubbling dish of enchiladas that looked like it had come straight from the oven. "I made them myself," Peter said, "Let's eat while it's hot."

Alongside the entrée, the table held dishes of rice, beans in some type of sauce, and a colorful salad smothered in freshly-grated cheese. Mixed aromas — spices, tomatoes, and smoky meats — filled the room, causing Carrie's stomach to growl. She heard Mig say, "Smells delicious," as she drew in a long, deep breath.

They passed the dishes around, filling their plates, and then digging in. Carrie was pleasantly surprised to find that the enchiladas were good-and-spicy. She and Mig had a habit of making food spicier than most, sometimes hotter than their extended family liked, and she guessed Mr. Braggin liked food as spicy as they did.

"This is as good as my Mom's was," Mig said at one point. Carrie agreed. The food smelled wonderful and tasted fantastic.

Speaking little as she ate, Carrie instead listened, observing as Peter — who kept insisting they call him by his first name — and Mig fell into easy conversation as they had on the previous visit. The men discussed the finer points of yard work, followed by fishing, and several unconnected topics, falling silent only when both took a bite of food at the same time.

Finishing her meal, Carrie leaned back. Nothing that they touched on seemed suited for an article, and she waited for Peter to disclose his reason for inviting them tonight. *He'll get to it soon*, she assured herself, although she was beginning to feel impatient.

After dinner, Peter suggested they move into the kitchen for coffee and dessert. Mig and Carrie helped clear the table and load the dishwasher. Peter had initially declined their help, as they were his guests, but Mig pointed out that they outnumbered him and were going to pitch-in. Relenting, Peter turned his attention to the coffee pot.

Carrie loaded the dishes as quickly as she could, partially aware of Peter removing something from the refrigerator. The scent of vanilla filled the air. Her anticipation grew, as she deduced that Peter wanted to discuss the dinner's purpose in the less-formal kitchen setting.

As the coffee pot brewed and hissed, Peter thanked them for cleaning up and urged them to sit, directing them to tall chairs along his kitchen island. He served Mig and Carrie slices of a white cake sopping with milk. "This *tres leches* cake is store-bought," Peter explained, looking slightly embarrassed, "but it'll be good with our coffee."

It was. The three ate dessert, drinking the strong coffee, and conversing between mouthfuls of the moist, sweet cake.

Noticing Peter's expression turning serious, Carrie swallowed her last bite and readied herself to take notes, discretely sliding her notebook from her pocket.

Mig had finished his cake, too, and said to Peter, "Thank you for dinner. It was fantastic."

"Yes," Carrie said. "Thank you for inviting us. This has been nice."

Peter held up his hand, "I'd like you to stay a little longer." His expression grew more serious, but his eyes were pleading, she thought, as if Peter feared their leaving, even though neither she nor Mig had stood.

Carrie glanced at Mig, who nodded and said, "Sure. We're staying, Peter. What's up?"

Carrie saw Peter's whole body relax. While Mig kept his expression neutral, Carrie fidgeted in anticipation of whatever newsworthy thing Peter was about to divulge.

"Thank you," Peter said. "I do have something I'd like to talk with you about. It's about time."

After a gulp of coffee, he continued. "I'm going to dive right in. When we met several years ago, you'll remember I was presenting on my time travel views and the ethics of changing the past. For practical purposes, I acted like a bit of a crackpot."

He paused. Mig motioned for him to continue without commenting. Carrie leaned forward.

"You see, I intentionally adopt some... um, extravagant personality traits, you might call them, to give the impression that I'm a bit mad. Unhinged, even. This ruse is necessary to ensure the wrong people don't take me too seriously. I don't mean *you* when I say the wrong people," he clarified, "I mean people who seek to use time travel to do very bad things, political or selfish things."

Peter held up one hand, palm out toward them, as if motioning for them to *stop*. When he spoke again, Carrie realized it had been to stop himself. "Let me back up for a moment. Mig, Carrie, before I say more, I must ask if you will keep our conversation 'off the record' and out of the news."

As he peered at each of them, they nodded. "Agreed," Mig said.

"Yes. Agreed," Carrie confirmed, although disappointed. So, the evening wouldn't yield an article, but her curiosity level soared, and she fought to keep her excitement from showing.

Peter nodded again before continuing, "I invited you two here because I wanted to confide in you that I can, and have, traveled through time."

He paused again. Carrie believed he was giving them an opportunity to respond, but she was speechless. This was far beyond anything she'd imagined, even knowing he spoke publicly on time travel ethics. *Does he really believe he can do such a thing? That's crazy.*

She looked desperately at Mig, whose eyes were wide. Disbelief showed on his face, and Carrie was sure it was showing on hers, too. Mig shrugged to her, then focused back on Peter, motioning for him to continue.

Peter nodded, now fidgeting himself, Carrie noted. "I'm telling you this for several reasons, and I'll explain, eventually. You'll understand why this must stay between us."

Carrie couldn't contain herself. More of a statement than a question, she blurted, "So, you have a... a haunted house, *and* you're a time traveler?"

Peter held out both hands palms-up. "If you'll be patient, I'm happy to explain. I promise that, given time, I can assuage your doubts about me."

When neither of them spoke, Peter stood, adopting a professorial tone and gesturing with his hands — intermittently running one through his mussy hair — as he continued. "Time travel works simply like this: an event is changed, people's actions redirected, and the timeline on which we live is replaced. A new sequence of events, within the sphere-of-influence of what I've corrected, takes its place upon the timeline. What I do is make small corrections for the benefit of others."

Pulling two boxes of matches from a drawer, Peter spilled them onto the counter. He pushed five blue-headed matches and a red-headed match into a line, head to tail.

"Imagine that this is the timeline we're on now. This red match represents our dinner tonight." Peter tapped the red-headed match.

"Why is it red?" Carrie asked. "Is it changed because you told us about time travel?"

"No. No, it's just a different color to represent where our dinner falls."

Mig interjected. "So, there's no *meaning* in its being a different color?"

"No. Um... My mistake. Let me start again. This is a lesson I've taught very rarely. Not the type of details I get into when I'm speaking publicly." Peter pulled the red-headed match away, replacing it with a blue-headed match. He cleared his throat, took a deep breath, and continued in a slightly exasperated tone, softer than the professorial one he'd been using. "So, these *six* blue matches represent a portion of our timeline. This fifth blue match is our dinner, and the sixth blue match is the current moment here in the kitchen."

He looked at them, then back at the matches, leaving no time for a response. "I could go back in time to our dinner," he pointed emphatically at the fifth match, "or even back to when I called and invited you," he touched the second match," and make it so I never told you about time travel. Do you follow me so far?"

This time, Mig jumped into the gap left by Peter's pause. "I'm with you. If you went back and changed those things, wouldn't a new timeline branch off? Isn't that how it works?"

Peter shook his head. "Not technically. At least, it would not be that way for anyone other than me, the time traveler, and even I perceive a single line. Anything not on it anymore is a faint memory to me and it doesn't exist for others."

Peter picked up a red-headed match and replaced the fifth blue match with it. Then, he picked up the displaced blue-headed match and struck it, letting it burn down to the wood before blowing it out. "This old part of the timeline goes away for everyone. All they'll know is the new version, represented by the blue-headed matches and the new red-headed one — where I've theoretically removed our dinner. The old piece is gone, with the exception that *I* will have a smoky memory of what had originally happened on it."

Carrie put her elbow on the counter, pressing her palm against her forehead. "Can you go over that again?" she asked, adding. "Please."

Peter replaced the red match with a blue one. He waved, a subtle Vanna-White-like motion, over the chain which again was made up of six blue-headed matches.

Peter repeated his explanation, pushing another red match into place and igniting the displaced blue match. "This represents the *previously experienced events*, replaced with my correction."

Holding up the just-burnt match, Peter said, "The old events leave a remnant with the time traveler, or travelers. The timeline with my corrections carries on, the change possibly affecting other future things, such as our being here in the kitchen. Only I remember how things used to be. It's like what happened before never happened as far as anyone knows. Well, except for me... and whomever stays inside my time travel room or travels with me."

"Wait a minute," Mig said, leaning forward and putting both hands flat on the kitchen island. "You have a time travel room?"

"Yes." Peter cleared his throat. "We'll get to that another time. For now, know that my traveling isn't about killing Hitler, or making big changes to the world, no matter how much I might want. I content myself with helping people by making corrections to their lives after a setback, in an attempt to remove whatever awful thing has happened to them. By focusing on small things, individual lives, families, I can make changes that do not ripple too far, nor change too much. This allows me to have a positive impact, one that *is* important to the person or persons involved."

Mig rose suddenly, carrying his empty mug to the coffee pot and refilling it. He motioned to Carrie and Peter with the pot, and Carrie handed her mug across for Mig to refill. Peter shook his head, then served a second piece of cake to each of them. Carrie took this as a sign he had much more to say.

Mig sat down on the tall chair again, handing Carrie her mug. She saw his hand was trembling slightly, and couldn't recall a time when anything had made that happen.

"All of this, I learned from my grandfather Alfonso. He showed me how time travel works, took me on trips, and left me to take over..." Peter trailed off. After taking a deep breath, he continued, "I'm the last of my family, the holder of our time travel knowledge. I see in you two the potential to *document* what I do. At a future point, if time travel is revealed to the world, my knowledge and warnings may serve others. Or, if that doesn't happen, we may preserve this knowledge merely for a future time traveler to hold in secret. I am hoping that, perhaps, you two will agree to be my preservationists. And, that you'll allow me to teach you as I make corrections, and even assist me in my work. Assistance is something I find myself needing. I won't get into that right now; but, does this interest you?"

Carrie stood quickly, realized she'd done so, and sat back down. She couldn't sort out her thoughts well enough to answer Peter's question.

"Why us?" Mig asked, breaking through the shambles of her thoughts. "You barely know us and you say you want to tell us your time travel secrets?" He looked expectantly at Peter.

Peter spread his hands out toward them again, his fork balancing precariously between two fingers. "Why you two? I think you two have the... character, for want of a better word, to help me do good things. Honest people are *not* a dime-a-dozen. It's rare I've come across a trustworthy person." He nodded toward Carrie, "Almost impossible to find two trustworthy people together, if you don't know this already.

"Mig, Carrie. I hope to show you many things, if you're willing. From what I've seen of the news you cover, I had an idea you might be open to this, and our visit last month gave me an opportunity to learn more about you both."

Mig took a long drink of coffee, his eyes averted into the mug. Carrie fiddled with her hands, her face contorting as she struggled with what Peter had shared.

After a hesitation, Peter added, "I'm a good judge of character. From what little I know of you both," he cleared his throat after what sounded like a lie and continued, "I believe I can trust you to keep my secrets."

Carrie drained her coffee mug without tasting it. Unnerved, a tumultuous battle raged in her mind. Part of her was shocked by the idea that the man in front of her thought he was a time traveler, another part of her wished she could laugh, and the rest of her wanted to grab Mig's hand and leave with him.

Mig asked question after question, nodding at Peter's responses. She listened, her mind growing fuzzier the more they talked. She wished she could concentrate on the conversation, as Mig seemed to be doing a good job of pulling information from Peter, but her head wouldn't clear. Several times she looked expectantly at Mig, hoping for him to notice her discomfort. His focus was on Peter, unfortunately for her.

Carrie stood suddenly. Floundering for a moment, she picked up her empty cake plate and walked to the sink with it. She busied herself cleaning it and adding it to the dishwasher, trying to clear her mind and ignoring the two men behind her. She could feel their eyes on her as she stretched out the washing of her hands as long as she could.

When she returned to the kitchen island, indecisive whether to sit again or remain standing, she saw Mig was up and pulling his car keys from his pocket. "I think this is a good time to call it an evening. Unless there's something else you want to add, Peter, I think Carrie and I are overflowing. How about we pick this up again another day?"

Peter rose and began walking toward the front door. "I understand. Just, please--"

"We'll keep it to ourselves. Don't worry, Peter. Thank you again for dinner." Mig shook Peter's hand, then put his hand on Carrie's back and followed her out the front door.

Carrie turned halfway around and said over her shoulder, "Please don't, um, burn our memories or anything, all right? Just give us a few days to take this all in."

Peter opened his mouth to speak, but she turned away and walked hurriedly to the car, yanking the door open hard enough to jar her shoulder, and dropping onto the passenger seat. As Mig waved and climbed into the driver's seat, she pulled her door shut, cutting off Peter in mid "Good-bye." Her heart thumped in her chest.

It was nearing 10 P.M. as they drove away from Peter's house. As they had the first time they'd met Peter Braggin, Mig and Carrie talked about him on the drive home.

Watching their taillights disappear, Peter thought, *That didn't go as I hoped.*

The problem, he believed, was partly their shock at his revelation, which he'd expected, and partly that he'd held back the rest of it. He'd decided mid-conversation that it was *not* the time to tell them he knew them well, but they can't remember. He'd traveled back in time and saved them when death had come calling. Those were long-gone events now only in *his* memory. Also, not a good ice breaker.

He'd faltered when he had lied about not knowing them well. Mentally, Peter kicked himself for not rehearsing what to say ahead of time. He had layers of smoky memories, from correcting the timeline where the Weathers were concerned.

He wondered — not for the first time — if he was slipping. Two failed trips to save Silvia Andrews, and now his imperfect planning for this important discussion. He shook off the thought, knowing he was still sharp in most regards, and young by time traveler standards.

More likely his fumbling, he knew, was due to his long reliance upon his grandfather to be his sounding board when he needed one. Even though Grampa had been gone for years, Peter still missed their long talks.

The man who had killed Silvia Andrews had gotten the drop on Peter, and it had unnerved him... the way his trips had fallen apart. For the correction he wanted to make, he had to get these new sounding boards in place, so he could work and plan with them.

Despite the awkwardness of the evening, Peter believed that he'd hear from the Weathers again. He believed, in the end, they would agree to help him.

By morning, Carrie's mind had mostly cleared. She and Mig started their day *almost* as usual — coffee and chatting. Except, all they talked about was time travel and what they believed the deal was with Peter Braggin. Was he crazy? Seeking attention? A hoaxer? Or, was he for real? Could he be for real? They discussed the many possibilities.

The subject dominated their discussions for days. While Mig went to see customers, Carrie wrote articles; but, each time they were together, the topics of Peter Braggin and time travel came up again.

Each time they talked, the idea of accepting his invitation to learn his secrets grew more enticing.

3 – Coffee Time

The following Monday, Mig showed Carrie an email he'd received from Peter Braggin, asking if they'd like to come over for coffee one morning. "I guess he figures he's given us long enough to think. We should go see him before he time travels and erases our dinner with him."

"Well, what's our answer? I don't think we've decided yet," Carrie said.

They discussed it again, and Carrie had to concede a point Mig made: that Peter probably wasn't dangerous, just eccentric. "Or, a time traveler. In which case, it's right up our strange alley."

"Tell him we'll come, then," Carrie said. "What have we got to lose?"

"Cool," Mig said. "How about tomorrow? I don't have any sales appointments until afternoon. Your schedule's flexible, right? Let's do it."

"Tomorrow morning, then," Carrie said, wringing her hands and ignoring a brief flutter in her chest.

Mig replied to the email, confirming they would stop by in the morning. He received a response from Peter immediately, inviting them to come over any time after 8 A.M.

Mig and Carrie arrived at Peter's house just before 10 o'clock the next morning, Carrie having taken an inordinately long time to get dressed — despite their wearing matching t-shirts with their news site's logo.

Peter greeted them, front door wide, with two mugs of hot coffee for them. As soon as he'd closed the door behind them, he led them down the stairs into his basement office. This was the room where Mig had photographed Peter's purported *ghostly presence*.

Peter motioned for the Weathers to sit in chairs in front of his desk, then asked if either of them had any questions about what he had said at their dinner together.

"So," Mig started, hesitatingly, which Carrie noted was unusual for him, "Why should we believe you're a time traveler?"

Right to the point, Carrie thought. *Good question.* She watched Peter closely, eager and nervous to hear his response.

Peter smiled and said, "Excellent question. And it tells me you've been thinking critically about what I've told you so far." He laughed. "And you likely discussed my sanity."

He paused, and Carrie resisted the urge to nod.

Peter continued. "I don't expect that you'll believe me right away. But I have much to show you. *When* you believe, then I am hoping you'll let me teach you some of what I know, document it, and change time with me.

"And, my planning skills have been off, so I could use extra eyes to pre-check my work. Some days, lately, I've been feeling my age, as the saying goes. I am glad to have you return and indulge me with the opportunity to convince you."

"Feeling your age?" Mig chuckled. "You look about the same age as me. We aren't *that* old."

Peter smiled broadly. "Looks can be deceiving for those of us who travel through time. I'll be 82 this year, though with all my travels I don't look it."

Mig and Carrie gaped at him, wearing nearly identical expressions of shock.

Ignoring their expressions, Peter said, "Now, to get to it... The haunted house photos you took in this office," Peter gestured around the room, "are actually photos of the residual energy emanating from my time travel room. I hope you will excuse my deception."

"What?!" Mig exclaimed more loudly than he usually spoke, startling Carrie. She watched as he pulled his smart phone out of his pocket and navigated to the photos he'd taken in Peter's office weeks prior. They'd published one with Carrie's article on the haunting.

Mig swiped through his photographs, zooming in on each, in turn. "What *was* that?" Mig asked, frowning at a zoomed in view of one photo, "What was that glow in my pictures?" Without waiting for a response, Mig walked past Peter's desk and stepped up to a section of the wall where his photo showed a glowing "apparition." He looked at the wall, then back at the zoomed photograph on his phone. Then, he looked to the floor and all around where he was standing. Carrie thought his behavior might have been comical if she wasn't so unnerved.

He asked Peter again, "What was it I photographed? Did you use hidden lights? Was it a projection trick?"

Peter walked to the wall near where Mig was standing. He looked at Mig, then reached out and pushed against the trim. Under his touch, a hidden panel clicked, then moved out toward his hand, revealing an opening where the ghostly aura had been positioned.

Mig moved back a step as Peter swung the panel open the rest of the way. Then, Mig stepped up to the opening in the wall, peering inside. "Whoa," he said.

Peter moved away and motioned for Carrie to come closer. Carrie walked over and stood next to Mig. They both leaned into the small room revealed by opening the panel. Filing cabinets and equipment lined one wall, with a long shelf full of knick-knacks along another. In the center was a lonely looking, old wooden chair.

They turned and looked at Peter.

"The source of the glow that appeared in your photos," Peter said, matter-of-factly. "No ghost, just energy from decades of traveling from inside there. This is my time travel room. Or, time machine, if you prefer," Peter said, raising his hands and making air quotes around *time machine*.

Peter squeezed past them with a "Pardon me," and motioned for them to enter the small room. Mig walked inside. Carrie hesitated, and then followed, stepping gingerly over the threshold as if avoiding an electrified wire.

"You won't *poof* off to another time," Peter said, not making fun of her, Carrie could tell, as he'd said it softly and kindly.

"This is not what I expected," Mig said, glancing around the space.

It's smaller than our dining room, Carrie thought. A faint smell lingered in the air. She couldn't place it, but it reminded her of holding her children as babies, fresh and clean. The scent didn't match the room, but made her feel warm inside, nonetheless.

Peter pointed to the shelf. It was loaded with many trinkets and the wood looked scratched. Carrie scanned the odd collection of small rocks, tiny carved figures, and various other items including an expensive-looking chess piece. Peter picked up the rook and handed it to Mig. "This object is a good one to use for a demonstration. I won't need it anymore, I think. It, like the other items on that shelf, is from one of my travels and shouldn't be here with me at this time. It can't exist outside of this space. Please, walk from this room out into my office. The ivory chess piece in your hand is going to disappear. I'm telling you in advance, so you two won't jump when it happens."

"Small room, not much space for jumping," Mig murmured. He held his left hand flat with the rook balanced on his palm.

He looks like he's offering a sugar cube to a horse, Carrie thought.

Mig walked forward to the threshold of the secret panel. Taking another step, he crossed into Peter's office. He was staring at his hand, as was Carrie, when a burst of darkness surrounded the rook, then seemed to eat the chess piece right off of his palm. In hardly a second, it was gone. Mig held his now-empty palm up toward Carrie, her mouth hanging open from the shock of watching the blackness eat the rook.

"*Poof,*" Peter said.

Mig held his palm toward Peter. "That's a heck of a magic trick."

Peter bobbed his head from side-to-side in a *maybe yes, maybe no* motion. "You can call it magic if you like. For me, it is merely what happens. It happened to the rook..." he pointed at Mig's empty hand, "and something *similar* happens to me when I leave on a trip to another time."

Carrie sniffed the air, then wrinkled her nose. "It smells like rotten apples now," she said. After another glance at Mig's empty hand, she stepped past him into the office and stood watching the men.

Crossing the threshold back into the small room, Mig turned his palm over slowly — as if expecting the white rook to reappear. "Not a haunting," Mig said in a low voice, addressing neither Peter nor Carrie directly.

"Yes, I'm afraid I deceived you about mine being a haunted house; but, I wanted to speak with the two of you again, and..." Peter shrugged his shoulders.

In a low voice, Carrie said, "I don't think there's any harm done." Her mind was racing with thoughts of H.G. Wells, and the fact this strange man could do things that shouldn't be possible; even, maybe, be a time traveler. Her stomach began to flip-flop.

A moment later, thankfully, their work moved to the forefront of her confused mind. "In fact," Carrie said, as she reached out and touched the panel's edge with her fingertips, "that article has been one of the most popular this month and, Mig, it isn't like we said it was a scientifically-proven ghost. I mean, our strange news is presented as strange, not hard fact, so I think we're good there. I'd even consider keeping it on the news site. Right, Mig?"

"Yep," Mig agreed, distractedly staring at a photo on his smart phone again, zooming in and out, then peering around the small room.

With a "Huh," Mig shoved his phone into his pocket. The logic of Peter's explanation of why they were there didn't make sense to him. Something else was going on.

One of the biggest secrets in the world — assuming Peter actually could time travel; it remained to be seen. That kind of secret information isn't just handed over to strangers. *No, it definitely isn't*, Mig thought.

To Peter, Mig said, "You invited us to see your, um, haunting," he put *haunting* in air quotes, "so you could find out if you could trust us, but we'd only ever had that one chat years ago at the expo..." He left the huge, unasked question hanging in the air. *You know us well somehow, don't you?*

"Yes." Peter stared back, giving no further elaboration.

Mig retreated to the office and Carrie saw his raised eyebrows and wide eyes without understanding why. She also noticed his golden skin had paled slightly.

She clutched for Mig's hand and squeezed. "Well, let's just see what else Mr. Braggin has to show us."

"Call me Peter, please," Peter intoned, stretching out the *please* as he joined them in the office and took his seat behind the desk.

Mig smiled wanly, winking at Carrie. A wink was one of the many ways he signaled *I love you*; or, in this instance she believed it meant, *I've got your back*; or possibly, *don't panic*. Carrie winked back at him, staring at the weak smile on his lips.

She returned to the chair by the desk, sitting down and facing the open panel and the time travel room beyond. Gesturing toward it with her chin, she asked, "Does that room really make time travel possible? Even with no machinery or blinking lights like in the movies?"

Mig strained to look into the little room again. Scanning for lights, Carrie assumed.

"Technically *I* make it possible," Peter said, now grinning like a schoolboy for some reason Carrie didn't understand.

"How many people know what you do?" she asked.

Mig chimed in, "Yeah, we aren't the first people to know you're a time traveler. We can't be, since you said you help regular people..." Mig paused, and Carrie saw the color draining from his face again before he added, "Who else knows?"

Peter pondered for a moment, then responded, "Me, my small family knew, you two, and a few people I've helped over the years whom I invited to remain in my time travel room while I corrected their problems." He gestured toward the open panel and explained, "When a person stays inside that secret room while I take a trip, they retain memories of how things were, their conversations with me about making a change, and, of course, they see the new reality after the correction.

"It has been few people. The vast majority of those I've helped have no memory something was changed in their lives. Depending on how they found me in the first place, they may not even remember me, or recognize me when we pass on the street. Honestly, that's easiest. Cleaner and safer, too."

Mig, staring at Peter, said, "I'm interested in what you're offering to share about time travel. I think Carrie would agree--"

"I'm interested," she interrupted, a shudder passing through her body as the implications of her words hit her.

Mig continued. "Before we become your archivists, or apprentices, or whatever you have in mind, can we talk with anyone you've helped? Or, watch you changing someone's life? I mean, the chess piece disappearing was cool and all, but you can't expect us to dive in without 'proof of life,' as it were, do you?"

"I think you mean proof of concept," Carrie interjected.

"I was trying to make a joke. I think Peter knows that." He shot a side glance at Peter, puzzling Carrie.

Peter had taken a drink of coffee, and at Mig's statement he choked. He started coughing, liquid dripping onto his desk. Coughing as he wiped off the desk top, he excused himself.

Peter walked down the hall to the bathroom, picked up a hand towel, and wiped the coffee off his chin and the front of his shirt.

Mig's use of the term, *proof of life,* had taken Peter by surprise, and he kicked himself for his reaction. The phrase was far too applicable. After all, Peter was having a conversation with two people who were there *because* he had time traveled to save each of their lives. Mig and Carrie's presence was proof of time travel.

Peter wasn't planning to tell the Weathers the entirety of their now-forgotten ordeals. At least, not yet. The unspoken bit he knew Mig had picked up was more than enough.

He'd stick with his plan, to show them a new correction, get them to believe, rather than shock them by announcing *they* were proof. Again, he chastised himself for not rehearsing what he would say before the Weathers arrived. *I can't be careless now*, he thought, seeing his determination in his reflection in the bathroom mirror.

Gathering his thoughts, Peter went back into his office and sat down in his desk chair. He made his apologies, cleared his throat, and made eye contact with Mig. "I propose a small test to give you proof of time travel. I want you both to understand that I'm a time traveler, not a magician, so we can move forward. Let's arrange for me to go back and change something minor. As I've done a few times with others, I'll ask you two to remain inside the time travel room while I go back to correct... *something*," he looked lost in thought for a moment, then added, "When you have memories of a correction, that should serve as proof."

"Okay. Sounds good," Mig agreed.

Peter noted that the color he'd seen drain from Mig's face had returned. That was good. Carrie was nervous enough; he didn't need Mig freaking out.

Carrie said, "Sure," but Peter thought her eyes looked a little too wide for her own good. He'd need to find a better approach if he didn't want to scare her away.

Peter stood. "All right, then. Let's go and see what we can find that happens today and needs to be changed. No time like the present. We can grab some lunch — my treat — if you have time right now.

"Now is good," Mig said.

Carrie nodded, though Peter thought she looked like a deer caught in headlights, not the confident reporter she'd been before his reveal at their dinner.

"Excellent," Peter said, tapping his palm against the desk top. Once we've agreed on what to change, we'll make a plan. Then, you'll come into my time travel room with me, say, tomorrow night, and I'll show you corrections in action. Now, let's go and see what's going on in downtown."

4 – Lunch Time

Carrie suggested lunch at a restaurant called Manny's Mexican Grill, to which Mig and Peter agreed. Mig and Carrie loaded into their car, Peter following in his own, and they headed off toward the Nash County restaurant. On the way, Mig called to postpone his afternoon customer meeting.

Ten minutes later, seated in Manny's, they each ordered tacos, nibbling on chips and salsa as they watched the sidewalk traffic through the restaurant window.

"What are we looking for?" Carrie asked. "Can you explain the kinds of things you change?"

"Yeah, we need an idea of what we're doing here," Mig said. "What are we looking for? What do you correct?"

Peter spoke in a low voice, "We are looking for someone who is having a bad day. At least, let's start with that in mind. Once we see something is going wrong for someone, we will look closely at it and plan a way to fix it."

Mig was looking at Peter, and Carrie noted the deep-in-thought expression on his face. She squeezed Mig's hand under the table. When he returned the squeeze, she whispered, "Are you all right?" He smiled at her, and Carrie saw his eyes were dark, unfocused, the smile forced. She assumed he had doubts, as did she, and made a mental note to talk with him about their doubts later.

The server approached and carefully placed hot dishes in front of them, then stepped away and returned with a pitcher to top off their drinks.

Carrie shook hot sauce onto her shrimp tacos — not her usual choice, but under the circumstances, trying something new seemed appropriate. She passed the sauce bottle to Mig. He added a few shakes of hot sauce to his carnitas tacos, and offered the bottle to Peter, who swiped it from Mig's hand.

"Thank you," Peter said, shaking quite of lot of sauce onto his meal; also carnitas tacos. "They never make the food hot enough in restaurants."

"True," Mig agreed.

"Mig and I like spicy food, like your enchiladas the other night," Carrie said, happy to be distracted from time travel for the moment. "We grow our own hot peppers, roast them, and Mig makes a tasty green chile. It's good and hot. Maybe we'll have you over for his chile some time."

"Excellent," Peter said, "I grew up eating spicy food. Those enchiladas had some of my own homegrown peppers in them. Maybe we can talk gardening and other normal things, once I've turned you into believers."

While they ate, Peter, Mig, and Carrie watched the street scene, restaurant staff, and the few other diners, looking for a person in trouble, an accident, or other event Peter could change to prove his time travel abilities.

Clueless, Carrie intently watched each person who walked by.

Nothing stood out. With no target found, they finished their lunch, Peter paid their bill, and they exited the restaurant. Mig shook Peter's hand and said, "Looks like today is a bust, Peter."

Peter raised his arms and shrugged, then walked with them to their cars. "We can try again another day. Will you give me another chance to provide proof?"

They agreed that, as soon as possible, they would meet again. "We're definitely giving you another chance," Mig said, fist-bumping Peter before climbing into the car.

Carrie waved good-bye as Mig drove them away from the disappointed-looking man. After circling the block to see if anything was happening around town, Mig drove them home.

That evening, Carrie lay on the couch, face tinged green. She said to Mig, "I think I have food poisoning." She groaned, wrapping a blanket over her hips and hugging her stomach.

"Aw, poor baby," Mig hugged her gently and slowly released her. "I feel okay, but I ate carnitas. You had shrimp, right? Seafood at an inland restaurant isn't always a good idea." He squeezed Carrie's shoulder, and rubbed her arm gently, concern showing on his face. "Can I get you anything?"

"A glass of water, please."

As Mig turned to walk away, she grabbed his arm. "Wait." Her eyes sparkled. "Can you get me a time machine? I need to go back and not eat the shrimp."

Mig's eyes brightened. "I guess we have our test after all! "I'll call Mr. Brag-- Peter right now."

"Oof, can you get me water first?" Carrie asked.

After getting her a glass of water from the kitchen and setting a roll of chewable antacids on the table beside her, Mig picked up his cell phone and dialed. When Peter answered, Mig said "We've got a test for you," and then explained how Carrie was ill with food poisoning from lunch.

Carrie heard the word, "Wonderful," coming through Mig's phone from Peter's side of the conversation. She pouted and hugged her stomach gently.

Mig — speaking back and forth with Peter on the phone and Carrie on the couch — arranged for the three of them to meet at 10 P.M. the next evening at Peter's house. Mig said good-bye and ended the call.

"Well," Mig said. "We're set for tomorrow night. Can you hold out until then?"

Carrie groaned, but raised her hand and gave Mig a thumbs-up.

In the middle of the night, Carrie's stomach woke her. She folded her arms across her middle and hugged, wishing for the pain to stop.

Then, she realized Mig was talking in his sleep. She couldn't make out what he was saying until he said, "Poof," and rolled over. After that, he quieted.

Carrie gently rubbed his back, then snuggled against him, her upset stomach gurgling.

5 – Testing 1, 2, 3

Carrie crawled out of bed in a grumpy frame of mind, having slept little. Mig must have seen it, as he gave her a soft kiss followed by a bear hug. He rubbed her belly gently. "I'm going to head out to work. I've got customers to see," he said. "Can I get you anything before I go?"

"Can't you stay home?" Carrie whined.

Mig gave her another hug and kiss, "I've got people to see. You rest. Take some medicine for your stomach. With luck, this time travel dude will fix you up tonight."

His eyes are sparkling. He thinks this is fun, Carrie thought. Then, she realized the idea of time travel sounded good to her, too. Anything that might make her gut better sounded good.

Slowly, Carrie walked to the front window and watched Mig drive away. Then, she spent the morning curled up on the couch, between hasty trips to the bathroom. The anxiety she'd been feeling since Peter's big reveal had waned. The possibility of time travel as an *undo* for her food poisoning filled her with hope. As her stomach squeezed, her breath catching, she hoped Peter Braggin was for real.

By the evening, Carrie was less queasy and her mood had improved. Mig and Carrie had plans to meet their kids for dinner. Carrie had considered staying home, but she wanted to see everyone as planned. She filled up on medicine before they headed out.

The Weathers had met and married later in life. They'd blended their families together — four children, pre-teen through adult, and three young grandchildren. All of the children were grown and out of the house now, with the youngest finishing college.

Carrie, Mig, and their family filled a long table at the back of the restaurant. Perico's food was passable and inexpensive; perfect for their group.

Carrie ate little, just enjoying the visit with the kids. Each of their adult children shared updates as Carrie listened happily. She was glad they were sharing a meal together, despite her sour stomach.

Grace, the youngest, caught them up on her college life-happenings. Son Dylan and his wife, Brianna, had married a few months prior, and they joyfully described their recent, chaotic move into an apartment on the other side of town. Middle-daughter Juli passed her phone around, showing off her and her husband Corvi's new flock of chickens. Oldest, Nicole, and her husband Greg raved about a Fall beach trip in the planning. Through it all, Carrie laughed, commiserated, and beamed proudly, all but forgetting her sickness.

Mig and Carrie had agreed in advance that they wouldn't mention the strange Mr. Peter Braggin. They had agreed to keep their time-travel discussions with him a secret. Since their only other recent encounter with him had been the haunted house article, they'd decided no mention of him was best. It would be one thing that they didn't share with their loved ones.

Carrie sipped at her water; the smell of food in the air nauseated her and sipping helped. She didn't mention being sick, as she feared that *if* Peter really could correct her food poisoning, his correction might impact their nice dinner.

Although she enjoyed their time together, Carrie was relieved when the meal was finished, and they exited Perico's

Restaurant. As they walked to their cars, the kids still chatting and laughing, she drew in deep breaths of the outside air, where the food smells were fainter.

After saying their good-byes and seeing the kids off, Mig and Carrie headed home, stopping at a drive-through for coffee on the way. As soon as they had drinks in hand, they resumed discussing Peter and the *what-ifs* of time travel as a reality.

Promptly at 10 P.M., Carrie and Mig arrived at Peter's house. He ushered them inside. "Time to go to work," he said, grinning at his own wordplay.

Peter sure loves saying the word time, she thought. Carrie suppressed a smirk and rolled her eyes for Mig. His eyes were wide open, sparkling with excitement.

She was excited, too, and knew they were both hoping for the impossible — that Peter Braggin was "for real" and they might see time change. Still, they had discussed the possibility they were going to be disappointed by the supposedly "old man" who claimed to pretend crazy, while they wondered if he wasn't actually crazy and only fooling himself. They were prepared for the disappointment more than they were for success.

Peter sat them down in his office and explained that his goal for the correction was to stop Carrie from ordering shrimp tacos and thereby avoid food poisoning. "Now, what will make Carrie change her mind about what to order?" Peter asked.

Mig made a few suggestions, knowing some of Carrie's food habits, and they agreed Peter would say something disgusting about shrimp, or ocean pollution, until the Carrie-back-then would order something else. Carrie hugged her stomach, made queasy by the mention of shrimp.

"Maybe I'll talk up the carnitas, since Mig and I didn't get sick," Peter suggested.

They made a plan for Peter to return to the prior morning, before they had met to talk and go to lunch. Peter explained he would leave a note for then-Peter to change Carrie's mind about what to order at the restaurant. Then, he would return to their time right away. "Which means you'll see me tomorrow morning."

"Can you explain that again?" Carrie asked.

"Of course. You two will stay here while I go back to yesterday morning," Peter explained. "You'll go to sleep in the time travel room, and mustn't leave for any reason. Then, you'll wake up in your own bed *tomorrow* morning. You won't feel sick, you'll have a clear memory in which you ate something else, plus smoke-like memories of eating shrimp and getting food poisoning. Mig will have the same two sets of memories. Your retention of memories from both versions of our meal will confirm my time traveling. That is, assuming Carrie listens to past-me and doesn't insist on ordering shrimp." A smile teased at the corners of his mouth.

Carrie shot back a weak smile. "I'm sure past-me will listen. Just make sure past-you talks up the carnitas really well, okay?"

"It'll help to say shrimp smells like dead fish. She's easily grossed out." Mig's face stayed serious as he said this, Carrie saw. *He's ready to believe Peter can time travel*, she thought. Then, she realized she was, too. The odd man's confidence was catching.

Peter scribbled for a moment on a pad of paper, then ripped off the top sheet. He asked each of them to sign the paper — which contained his notes on the why and how of the trip to come — before carrying it into the time travel room and placing it on top of a file cabinet. "Okay, all set. The paper needs to be in here, just as you two do."

Mig followed Peter through the open panel into the tiny room. Carrie followed, again stepping gingerly over the threshold. They stood together near the wooden chair in the center of the room.

Peter shrugged and said, "It might be uncomfortable for a short time, as you cannot leave the room and must go to sleep while I take my trip to leave a note about our lunch for myself," Peter made air quotes around *myself*. "Once you fall asleep, you'll wake up in your own bed tomorrow morning. If I've succeeded with this change we've discussed, then you two will remember everything, just as I will. Come and see me tomorrow, hopefully Carrie will be feeling perfectly healthy, and we'll talk about it."

Carrie shot a nervous glance at Mig. He must have seen the worry in her eyes, as he said to Peter, "Excuse us a minute."

He and Carrie moved out of the room to talk out of earshot of Peter. "What if he does something while we're sleeping?" Carrie asked.

Mig squeezed her hand. "I'm a light sleeper. But, I doubt he's going to do anything to us. I trust him, okay? There's something genuine about him, and you know I'm pretty good at figuring people out. That's why I'm the super salesman," he teased, giving her a quick peck on the lips.

Carrie relaxed, returning a peck, "Okay. If you think it's safe..."

Mig nodded and promised, "Whether we wake up in this room, or back at home like he says we will, I'll make sure we both get strong coffee tomorrow morning."

Rubbing her stomach, Carrie agreed. "Hopefully coffee will sound good by then."

As they returned to the time travel room, Peter urged them to visit the bathroom one more time, then he closed the panel shutting the three of them in. "You mustn't leave this room once I go back on my trip. If you're out of the room when the timeline changes, you won't *poof*, but your memories will be affected. Let's not chance it. I want you to have your proof when you wake up tomorrow. Then, we can move forward."

Carrie leaned against Mig, feeling anxious. The contact with him calmed her.

Peter pointed toward the far corner. "I've left you two blankets and pillows which may be a comfort against the hard floor. Do not leave the room. Go to sleep, even if it's difficult. But do not leave this room."

"We won't," Mig assured him. "Just do what you need to do, and we can talk tomorrow."

"Good. Go ahead and settle in. Stay out of my line-of-sight and quiet, please, as I must concentrate to go." He put air quotes around *go*.

They moved to the corner. Mig helped Carrie lower herself, then he slid down the wall to sit beside her on the stack of bedding.

"Carrie, you may continue feeling the aftereffects of your illness after I leave, but if all goes well, you will fall asleep quickly and wake up with no sickness. Never having been sick."

Carrie looked at Peter, then at Mig, then nodded as she patted her belly. It twisted, not only from the last vestiges of food poisoning, but her rising fear at what might be about to happen. Peter seemed so sure of himself...

After apologizing again for the discomfort of the floor, Peter sat down in the chair at the center of the room. Mig and Carrie watched him moving items on the shelf, and heard him take several deep breaths. Then, Peter dissolved in a cloud of sparkling blackness, leaving the empty chair in the center of the room, and reviving the scent that reminded her of new babies.

"What the hell?" Mig exclaimed.

"I can't believe it!"

"He freaking disappeared." Mig's voice rose at the end, his statement sounding like a question.

After minutes of silence, he added, "I guess he isn't crazy."

Mig and Carrie stared at the chair, the soothing, infant-reminiscent scent wafting around them. In a low voice, Carrie posed the questions of whether it was possible that this strange man had drugged them, or if they really were time-travel adjacent. "I think we'll know more in the morning."

To lighten the mood, Mig made a joke about Peter's constant repeating of instructions as if they were small children. Carrie smiled, starting to be more hopeful than afraid.

Soon after Peter's departure, the scent increased and enveloped them. They stopped talking and dozed off; Carrie first, holding tightly to Mig's hand, and seconds later, Mig, with his other arm draped over her.

6 – Proven

The following morning, Carrie awoke at home in bed. She rolled onto her side to face Mig, and met his eyes, wide open. He smiled, said good morning, then bolted upright. "Wait a minute. What happened?"

Carrie gasped as memories of the night before flooded her mind. She sat up, gripping Mig's right arm with both hands.

Mig looked at her, eyes narrowed. "Do you remember being in that weird room?"

She nodded. "Peter puffed out like a... like a candle or something..." Carrie said, looking at Mig questioningly. "Like nothing I've seen before. It was way weirder than the thing with the rook. How did he do that? Where did he go? What do you think?"

Mig frowned and, instead of answering any of Carrie's questions, said, "I should feel funkier." He asked Carrie, "How do you feel, sweetheart?"

Carrie gasped again. "The food poisoning!" She touched her stomach, then began pushing hard onto it. She asked Mig to push on her belly too. "I feel... well."

"Wow." Mig said, looking much calmer than Carrie thought he should be, much calmer than she was.

"Wow, for sure! I thought I'd feel blah for days but I'm all right. The thought of eating shrimp doesn't even make me queasy."

Mig's brow furrowed. He shook his head, biting at his upper lip, lost in thought.

"Wait a minute!" Carrie thought for a moment. "I clearly remember eating carnitas when we went to lunch, after Peter made that comment about how shrimp were found contaminated with pesticides and oil after hurricanes.

"I also remember eating shrimp tacos and getting sick; though, the shrimp memories are more like I dreamed them." She looked at Mig.

"I remember both lunches, too," Mig said. He climbed out of bed, stood up, and tossed the comforter over her head playfully. "Let's go see the man."

Carrie escaped the coverings, rolled across his side of the bed, and hopped down, landing on her feet next to him just in time for him to lean down for a kiss.

They dressed quickly, neither taking the time to shower.

Mig called to postpone an appointment scheduled that afternoon with a long-time customer. Carrie overheard him promising to stop by soon, then thanking the customer for extending his advertising another six months.

Health and wealth. Today's starting pretty good, she thought.

The Weathers drove straight to Peter's house without calling ahead, nor taking time for the planned strong coffee. It was 8 A.M. and they were going to see the time traveler.

They were halfway to Peter's when Mig asked again, "How do you feel?"

Carrie pressed on her stomach, pushing at it several times before declaring, "I feel fine. It's like I was never sick."

Mig furrowed his brow. "Maybe you just feel better because another day has gone by," he offered. "Let's not get crazy about this until we understand what happened. Okay?"

"Yeah, I agree. But I gotta tell ya, Mig, the double-memory thing has me pretty convinced. It's nothing like *déjà vu* or anything I've experienced before. Not to mention, we never left that room, made the drive home, or went to bed, yet we woke up at home."

As Mig parked on Peter's driveway, Carrie saw Peter waiting at the door for them. She did her best to walk nonchalantly up the sidewalk, failing to do so, although Mig succeeded. Peter turned and led them into his kitchen. "So, what did you two do last night?" he asked, grinning broadly.

Carrie was confused for a moment, wondering if he didn't remember them sleeping in his time travel room. Mig replied, "Nothing special," and she realized each of the men was deflecting, wanting the other to confirm the previous night's events. *Men*, she thought, rolling her eyes.

An amused expression on his face, Peter said, "Well, I'll go first then. Are your legs cramped from sleeping on the floor in my time travel room?"

"Not at all cramped, and neither is my stomach," Carrie blurted.

Mig's tone was serious as he said to Peter, "It's a little freaky, but I remember two versions of our lunch."

Carrie's eyes wide, her voice quavered slightly as she said, "So do I."

Peter nodded. "What did you have for lunch when we met at the restaurant, Carrie?"

"I remember having the carnitas. They were so good. That memory is sharp. I also have a hazy memory of eating shrimp tacos and being sick, but those memories are dream-like."

"Mig, are those the same as the two memories you have?"

"Yep. It's like you said it would be."

Peter tapped the counter with his hand. "Good! So, I think we can agree you have your proof. Mig, Carrie, you can be sure from what you have experienced, proven by your two types of lunch memories, that I indeed traveled in time. You could even go to the restaurant, and the server would remember

Carrie eating carnitas with us. That is, if you don't trust your own memories and want more evidence."

"I think we agree that our extra memories are proof you time traveled." Mig said, adding, "Peter, how did your trip go?"

Peter said, "Perfectly, based on the result."

"What now?" Carrie asked.

"Now, I think now we should set a schedule for me to pass along to you what I know. Yes?"

"Yes," Mig and Carrie said together.

"Excellent! When can we meet? What are your Saturdays like?" Peter flipped open the calendar app on his cell phone.

The three of them arranged to meet on the coming Saturday to start Peter's knowledge transfer.

When Mig and Carrie returned home, Mig dropped onto the couch, sinking into the cushion. "Wow."

"I know. Crazy," Carrie said as she flopped onto the cushion next to him.

Silence stretched between them for minutes.

Carrie blew out a breath. "Wow, this is the best story we've ever had, and we can't report it."

Mig tilted his head back, resting it against the couch top. "No, we can't. That's for sure." After a pause, he added, "But with the possibilities it opens up, it's better people don't know. I'm glad to know, though, and I can't wait to learn how. Can you imagine? It's like a superpower."

"Kind of scary," Carrie said softly.

"Yep. I know what you mean. Cool as heck, though."

"Wow," Carrie said again. Then, she nudged her husband. "Now, how about that coffee you promised, Mig?"

***

The rest of Mig and Carrie's work week proved incredibly mundane compared to their brush with time travel.

Carrie could see Mig's excitement building as Saturday approached. This wasn't stalking through the woods looking for Bigfoot or watching the skies for unidentified flying objects. Time travel's possibilities exhilarated and frightened her.

7 – The First Lesson

On Saturday, seated in Peter's office, the time traveler asked Carrie and Mig to relax while he spoke. "I need you to bear with me as I try to pass along what I know, what I learned from my Grampa.

"I'll do my best to present time travel logically, ethical implications included, of course. I believe you'll be able to travel with me once you know the basics. I'll fill in gaps as you begin helping me make corrections."

Mig laughed. "It's our first time learning how to jump through time, so we'll all have to cut each other some slack."

"I haven't been in a class in a long time, "Carrie said. "I'm happy to listen and take notes. I'll ask questions when I'm confused. That'll be a lot of the time," she said, kidding but not.

Peter took a gulp of coffee and swallowed hard before continuing. "We'll begin here in my office. I want to start with the basics: concentration, breathing, and so on. Then, we'll move on to focusing on the *wheres* and *whens*.

"After that, I'll take you into the time travel room and we'll repeat the lesson. The collective energies in the room, from my use and my grandfather's, provide a boost."

Mig asked, "Are you saying you can travel without being in that room?"

"Yes," Peter said, "but I don't. All my files and such are there, Grampa's too, and so I use it consistently. Besides, it's one thing to go back in time and worry about a stranger seeing me appear, quite another to pop-off in my backyard and risk someone who knows me screaming as I disappear — even though I can undo it."

"Good point. What happens if I can't concentrate well enough to travel?" Carrie asked. "Or if my mind wanders for a split-second? Will I end up in the wrong place?"

"Coming out the wrong place or time can happen. Certainly, when I began traveling on my own, I wasn't always standing exactly where I had planned to be, but I was always near to the right place and within minutes of the right time. My grandfather had made sure I was well-educated before he sent me out on my own. Trust me. I'll ensure we travel safely, and I can keep all of us together."

Peter coached them for an hour, him describing familiar locations around town while they practiced concentrating. Peter started with Manny's where they'd had lunch; next asking them to focus on the century-old downtown Town Hall's unique front entrance. With neither of the Weathers feeling anything in particular, Peter suggested they move the lesson into the time travel room.

They followed Peter through the panel and into the room. "Maximum efficiency in minimal space," Peter said, as he took time to carefully explain his filing system, unlocking and opening several file drawers.

He showed them a file from one of his recent trips. It was mandatory, he told them sternly, to write notes on every trip — before and after. "I write what is, what's to be corrected, my plan. When I return, I add the results. These records let me not only keep the details fresh in my memories, but allow me to review and learn from my mistakes. You'll find this process useful, too. This room holds all my notes and such safely, and can hold yours, so they don't disappear, regardless of corrections made."

Carrie stepped past the wooden chair in the center of the room, and approached the adjacent shelf of trinkets. Peter explained how he used them to concentrate only, and that the objects themselves contained no power.

Picking up a pink, plastic spoon, a wry smile crossed Peter's lips. "This one..." He rolled his eyes, "Oh, the arrogance of youth. Back in 1963 when I was in my mid-twenties, I saw a notice for a high school crush's wedding in the paper. Without Grampa's knowledge, I went back in time to a day I'd seen her on the street. Being in high school then, I'd wanted to ask her on a date but hadn't had the nerve. So, I waited for shy-me from then to walk away... I looked so dejected. I approached Kelly... Kelly Martin was her name and asked if she'd like to go out. She smiled. Oh, that smile." He looked wistful for a moment.

"Anyway, she said she was going for ice cream and invited me along. We had ice cream, talked a while, and then she dropped the bomb that she had a boyfriend. We went our separate ways.

"The next morning, though, Grampa busted me. He said he knew I'd used the time travel room, and I told the whole truth. Grampa was livid. Said I could have messed up the timeline, and made me check the paper to make sure her wedding was still on. Thankfully, it was, and to the same man. Big lesson for me. I got a tiny bit smarter after that." Peter chuckled, shaking his head.

Mig shrugged. "Everybody makes mistakes when they're young and dumb."

"True. True." Peter set the spoon back on the shelf. "I actually picked up the little pink spoon several years later. I went for ice cream, had the same strawberry scoop I'd had with her, and brought home that little spoon just as a reminder. Plus, it was the first time I'd seen one and, well, it's different."

He ran through the short versions of time-travel adventures for other objects — where he had picked each up, its meaning to him, including a dried flower with few remaining petals from a trip he and his grandfather had taken. That had involved merely getting a man into a cab so he made it to his daughter's birthday party. "This flower had been a bright blue," Peter explained, "and I plucked it from the street where it had fallen off of a bouquet that man had been carrying. Not the best choice of object, and I haven't used it for traveling." He held it out toward Carrie. "I don't need it. Would you like to walk into my office and watch it vanish, as Mig did with the chess piece?"

Carrie shook her head. "No, thank you."

Mig reached out for it. "I'll do it."

Peter dropped the dry flower in Mig's hand, and waited as Mig stepped into the office, and short-laughed as the sparkling black removed it from his hand. He stepped back into the time travel room with a grin.

"Ugh, the rotten fruit smell again." Carrie pinched her nose, shaking her head at Mig, but she was smiling.

"Envisioning where and you will go and when is all about the mind. Having something in your hand is merely a physical object to center yourself, should you wish to do so. Sometimes, I've run a fan in my office, too, for background noise. My Grampa would brew tea and put the mug on the shelf. He said he'd focus on its scent. Whatever it takes," he waved toward them, "for both of you to concentrate."

Pushing the wooden chair to one side, Peter repeated the focusing exercises. He started with the door of the Town Hall, adding more and more sensory details — sights, sounds, and smells. *He paints a vivid image*, Carrie thought, as she imagined the building's stonework, traffic moving by, heat coming off the asphalt parking lot, and smells of the flowering trees surrounding Town Hall. Despite this, her progress was nil, and she took to gripping different trinkets from Peter's shelf as she tried, to no avail.

"Feels the same to me in here as it did out in the office," she said, sighing.

Mig commented that he found concentrating inside the time travel room easier.

Mid-afternoon, all three were exhausted. Carrie declared her brain was full.

Peter suggested they meet for another session and lunch at his house on next Saturday. They agreed to call it a day, and the Weathers headed home.

***

At home that evening, Carrie found Mig standing in front of the living room windows, staring out at the darkness. She called his name, and he turned. Seeing the far-away look in his eyes, she asked, "What's wrong?"

"Nothing." He moved to the couch and sat.

"Seriously, what's up?" She took a seat beside him, touching his arm.

Relenting, Mig said, "I was just thinking. Hearing Peter talking about his Grampa and all, it got me thinking about my grandparents. The biological ones I never knew."

"Oh," Carrie said. She hugged him. She knew he often wondered about his mother Lina's family. Lina had been orphaned at a young age and adopted by a distant cousin of her mother's, who hadn't known Lina's parents very well. While Mig's mother had shared with him everything she remembered about her parents, as young as Lina had been when they'd died, there had been little to share. Carrie had found few new details in researching the family for him, as young Lina's movements were nonexistent in Census records.

"Carrie, can you imagine? The impossible... with time travel it's possible for me to meet my grandparents."

"You're right," Carrie said as she rubbed his shoulders. Then, the tension suddenly left them.

"I think Peter would be willing to time travel with us to meet my grandparents. You know, without telling them who we are."

She hugged him tight. "Ask him."

They stayed entwined, Mig pondering, and Carrie listening to his heart beat.

He stirred and she released him. "How about some tea? I think Peter gave us a lot to think about today. We should talk about it."

He went to the kitchen and poured two tall glasses, stirring a little sugar in hers. Mig returned to the couch and, after handing Carrie her tea, sat down. She faced him, her legs curled under her.

They drank their teas and discussed the lessons of the day, soon moving on to the potential of time travel.

Carrie mused, "So, a small correction is better than a big one, according to Peter. No trip to kill Hitler. No going back to stop dictators or anything like that."

"Nope." Mig set down his glass. Carrie could almost hear gears spinning in his head. His fingers played along the rim of the glass.

Carrie had a thought, though she knew it wasn't a good one, and said, "What about going back a year or two and giving free advertising to that wing joint? I know you and the kids wish it hadn't closed."

Mig laughed, then shook his head. "No, who knows what else was going on with them closing. And I think they're happy being retired, anyway."

"Yeah, you're right. Plus, it seems like a lame thing to change with something as powerful as time travel."

Mig nodded slowly. "It's powerful, all right."

"We could go back and avoid having the car hit by that truck in the mall parking lot last year," Carrie offered.

Mig laughed. "Nah, we've already done all the insurance paperwork and stuff. And besides, we went to see the kids afterward and borrowed their second car. I'd hate to lose that evening with the kids," Mig said, his brow furrowing.

Carrie gasped. "Wow, I hadn't thought about other stuff being affected."

Mig thought for a moment, and Carrie saw a dark expression cloud his eyes. Mig put his hand on Carrie's leg. "Look, I need you to not freak out, but I think Peter met us at the expo on purpose... Maybe I'm reading too much into it, but I feel like he knows more about us than he's saying. If he does know us somehow, I don't know... but I'm wondering if he said what he said back then to make sure my cancer got caught quick."

Carrie didn't freak out, which surprised her as much as it did Mig. "That seems incredibly logical to me. I should freak out, but... If it's true, then I'd be happy he did that for you. For us."

Carrie fell silent, drinking tea as the implication sunk in.

Mig squeezed her leg, then released it and flashed a forced, closed-lips smile. "Why don't we give it a rest and have some dinner."

Carrie sighed. "A break sounds good."

"Besides," Mig said, "we've only had one Saturday with Peter. We can't expect to find problems to solve already. We'll come up with better ideas *over time*."

Cringing at Mig's new habit of stressing the word *time*, something Peter did frequently, Carrie picked up her tea and headed into the kitchen.

She whipped dinner together quickly — spaghetti with hot Italian sausage in jarred sauce. As she cooked, she thought about the few notes she'd taken that day, thinking she should add to them, for posterity, and maybe pen a list of questions to ask Peter, such as the impact of changes on their time with their kids.

In short order, they were seated in the living room with full plates. No dinner table tonight; instead, they relaxed on the couch through dinner and beyond, the TV ignored, and bantered about their new, secret knowledge.

By the time Carrie called it a night, Mig was firing off puns and jokes about time and overusing the phrase, *life-changing*.

With Halloween mere weeks away, Mig and Carrie stayed busy and time flew by. Local haunted houses, corn mazes, and other activities needed to be reported on, and spooky activity lists posted. Carrie spent her days gathering details, and for selected events Mig had to go and take photos for the news site. Mig also had customers to visit. Fall was a busy time for advertising, with towns promoting fall festivals, and shops preparing for upcoming holiday sales.

Mig frequently invited one of the kids or a grandchild to come along when he was taking photographs, or while Carrie was interviewing the owner at an attraction. She and Mig loved having the "kiddos" along, and making the most of their family time — especially now that Peter would take up most of their Saturdays.

Before they knew it, Saturday arrived.

8 – October Surprise

The second Saturday in October, Mig and Carrie arrived mid-morning at Peter's house for another time-travel session.

They called their meetings *lessons*, but they consisted of Peter imparting his knowledge, Carrie taking notes, and Mig asking question after question. Although not a trained archivist, Carrie did her best to create a record of Peter's work; one that might never have readers beyond the three of them.

As the Weathers exited their car, Peter called to them from the top of the driveway and invited them to join him on his patio. The sun was shining, the air warm, and Peter had iced teas waiting on the patio table as they descended the stone steps into his tree-screened back yard.

As soon as they sat down, Peter began. "Since you're going to be involved with changing time, and you know how I feel about ethics, I've written down my rules for you." He handed a paper to Mig, then turned and handed its mate to Carrie.

"These are my rules. Well, there may be others. I've not written them down before. Anyway, we will follow them and plan each correction thoughtfully. I believe you'll find with these few constraints, many issues can be avoided."

The list included eight rules:

1. No military or government-related trips.
2. No trips to save the very young, only older children and adults.
3. Don't help anyone in love with money/power.

4. Avoid trips related to family.
5. Don't travel out of anger/revenge.
6. Get the facts beforehand.
7. Think of what others need, not what they want.
8. Correct only in a way you can live with.

"Your list is pretty short," Mig commented.

Peter leaned forward, elbows on the patio table, and motioned with his arms as he talked — almost tipping his tea in the process; Carrie caught it before it could spill. "This list covers many situations, despite its length."

He pointed to the third item on the list Mig was holding. "On number three, Mig, you are a good judge of character. You'd need to be, since you're working in sales. Your ability to size people up will serve you well in figuring out a person's intentions, and determining those who *should not* be helped using time travel."

Carrie slid her copy of the list across the table toward Peter. "Number two, um, about trips to save people of different ages. Does that mean what I think it means? Do you... can you... bring back people who died?"

"What?" Mig said, re-reading his list. "Whoa. How about it, Peter? Can you?"

Peter didn't answer right away. He looked at Mig and Carrie, opened his mouth to say something, then clamped it shut. After a minute of looking like he was doing an impression of a goldfish, he answered hesitatingly. "Yes. It's a significant correction to a timeline, but can be done. We can help someone by stopping a loved one's death from happening; if it's possible, that is. An accident can be corrected, but not all deaths can be. Even so, we need to be cautious and selective.

"When the very young pass away, well, a baby is on the timeline only briefly. I prefer to help those who have more established lives along the timeline."

"Dang," Mig and Carrie said together. Carrie pulled the paper back, and re-read the rules again.

Mig blew out a breath. "Carrie and I talked about hypothetical time changes, but I think we barely scratched the surface."

Carrie nodded. "I agree. We were... are clueless." She thought about asking if Peter had traveled to help Mig catch his cancer, then decided if Mig hadn't mentioned it, it was best not to ask.

The Weathers sat silently, re-reading Peter's list. After a few minutes, Mig broke the silence. "This list reads to me like a list of don'ts," he said, raising an eyebrow at Peter instead of asking a direct question.

"It is," Peter agreed. "I don't have a to-do list. When I see something I'd like to correct, or when someone comes and asks me for my help, I consider that specific context, and what ripples might be caused. I don't believe there is *ever* a requirement or *to-do* because in my opinion it's always okay to *not* make any corrections. To do nothing."

Carrie furrowed her brow. "Peter, would you be willing to tell us more about things you've changed, um, corrected, as a way to help us understand? Maybe if you tell us about trips you've taken for people and why you chose to take them... I think... maybe if I... we... had a better idea of what you've done..."

Mig summarized her awkward question, "Would you tell us stories about the many travels of Peter Braggin?"

Peter grinned from ear-to-ear. "Yes. Absolutely. I have many. And, I'm happy to have people to tell them to without posing them as hypothetical, or mixing in *ifs* and *maybes* as I must do when I speak at conferences."

"I know you present and all, but how often do you actually make corrections?" Carrie asked. "I can't imagine using time travel every day. I mean, in retrospect, I feel like us asking you to use *time travel* for my *food poisoning* was excessive."

"You wanted proof, and I made the choice. Don't feel bad, but, yes, it was overkill for the situation. We must all use time travel wisely. I'll share my stories as examples, and trust you to stick to my rules."

"I guess I understand what you expect of us, from your rules," Mig said. "I get that you want us to document your ability for posterity, but, with all the power you have, what do you gain by involving us?"

"What I get out of it is help. There will be things I can't do alone and I'll need your help."

Carrie saw Mig's expression change, puzzlement to suspicion, before returning to puzzlement. "I can live with that," Mig said, glancing at Carrie, "hopefully Carrie can, too. But, Peter, don't keep us in the dark too long.

"Agreed!" Peter said, exuberantly slapping his hand on the top of the chair. "So, let's get to it! I'll help you practice concentration and visualization inside the time travel room, as we went over in our previous lesson. When you can concentrate, I will teach you to move through time alongside me. So, let's get you both focusing."

"I'll try not to daydream," Mig joked.

Carrie rolled her eyes. "Oh my gosh, you have laser focus when you're working on something. I'm the daydreamer."

Mig laughed. "Peter, she's right about that. You should hear when we work on a news story. I'll be listing questions we should ask of an interviewee, and she'll be, like, 'Can we stop for milk on the way home?' She can think a dozen things at once." Carrie looked at him sideways, and he squeezed her hand. "Which is a feature, not a bug, sweetheart."

"Aw, thank you. I think." Carrie faced Peter. "I'm sure Mig's single-mindedness is going to be priceless."

"Wait," Mig said, "What if your brain is different from our brains, Peter? What if we can't use time travel the way you can?"

Peter waved off Mig's concern. "My grandfather never mentioned anything being special about us. He just started training me when I was a teenager, so I've had decades to hone it. I don't know of any reason why you two can't do this."

"Do you know that Stephen Hawking once held a party for time travelers?" Carrie asked, taking a turn from what they'd been discussing.

Mig laughed, "Case in point. Her mind is a treasure trove of information, and you never know when she'll get sidetracked. Okay, Carrie, when was that?"

She shrugged. "I don't remember when it was. I know a little about a lot. You know that. And I think it's relevant to this discussion, even if it is a tangent," she said, pouting.

Mig cocked his head to the side. "Maybe," he teased.

Peter folded his fingertips together in a peak, tapping them against his chin. He said, "Stephen Hawking was a highly intelligent man. I remember him holding a reception for time travelers, but he didn't announce it until after the date. His reasoning was that if he invited them afterward, only real time travelers could go back and join him. He ended up at the reception alone, which to him meant there were no time travelers."

"Why didn't *you* go?" Mig asked.

Peter laughed. "Even to a man such as Stephen Hawking, it would not have been prudent to expose myself."

Carrie asked, "Are there other time travelers? If so, why do you think no other travelers showed up?"

"For the same reason I didn't go, I imagine." Peter threw up his hands. "If there *are* others. Anyway, getting back to the possibilities here... If you two learn time travel, but we find that you can't travel without me, then we'll know. Let's assume it's possible for you, for now. Are you ready to continue?"

Carrie blew out a breath. She looked at Mig.

Mig nodded and said, "Let's give it another shot. It'll be awesome if we can do this."

"Worst case," Carrie shrugged, "we get to learn about it. I can add it to my mental treasure trove, right, Mig?"

Mig rolled his eyes, then nodded.

Peter walked them through concentration exercises in the small room. For each attempt, he described a place, gave a specific date and time, and asked them to focus as he filled in details. He started with the Town Hall entry as he had on a prior lesson, describing a recent holiday event on the Town Hall green that he knew Mig and Carrie had covered. Not having ever been to that particular town event, he fumbled in his description — Carrie interrupting him with, "There wasn't a petting zoo there" — and he restarted.

Carrie thought, *This is more like meditation than anything. Or hypnosis, perhaps*, although she'd only seen it on TV, never first-hand.

Carrie tried, but the more she failed, the more relief she felt. She realized how anxious she was about poofing off, getting lost alone in time.

By late afternoon, Mig was seated on the time travel room chair with Peter beside him, and Carrie was leaning against the wall.

"Once more, and we'll call it a day," Peter said.

"Come and try with me," Mig said.

"I'll just watch this time," Carrie said, though she hadn't participated the last few times either. "Maybe I'll just be more of a sidekick. You two go ahead, and don't worry about me poofing."

Peter shot Carrie a strange look, then his expression softened. "Okay, if you wish, Carrie," Peter said. "Research is your superpower and you can contribute in that way. I was my Grampa's researcher, but it was not something I liked to do. I'm more than happy to have you take that on."

"Okay, Mig," Peter said. "Listen to me carefully. Concentrate on the three of us standing outside Manny's Mexican Grill on the day we had lunch together." Peter described the sidewalk, the smells as they opened the restaurant door, the warm sun on their backs, and the empty tables around their seats.

Mig focused, following Peter's directions, and suddenly, Carrie saw Peter push his hand onto Mig's shoulder. "You're getting it. Excellent!"

Carrie couldn't tell what Mig had done, but her heart skipped a beat. "What happened? What's going on?" she asked Peter, but he was focused on Mig.

"I'm okay," Mig said.

Peter leaned back against the wall. Gesturing with one hand, he said, "Mig, concentrate hard while I paint the scene one more time. With the way you're progressing, you may start to travel there; but, I am ready to stop you before that happens. Okay?"

Mig nodded. He took a deep breath and blew it out slowly.

"Once more, right now," Peter said.

Mig concentrated as Peter described the restaurant scene again.

Suddenly, Carrie saw flashes, like sparks of darkness. Peter's hands were immediately on Mig's shoulder.

Mig's eyes shot open. Peter said, "Mig, look around this room. Focus on my voice. Let thoughts of the restaurant go. Look at Carrie. The only thing that stopped you from taking a trip into the past is me. Let go of the scene you were visualizing, and focus on us, here, in this room with you."

"Wow," Mig said. "For a split-second, I thought I saw the restaurant in front of me. Feel my heart, Carrie. It's pounding."

Peter laughed. "You're a fast learner. Good. This is excellent. Surprising, but excellent."

Carrie stepped forward, reaching for Mig, but found her hand hesitating. She was afraid to touch him.

64

9 – Role Playing

As Peter walked them to their car, he stressed that Mig be careful not to practice the concentration exercises without Peter being present. Mig assured him that he had no intention of doing anything without Peter to guide him.

As they climbed into the car, Peter reminded them to be careful where they discussed time travel, and asked that Carrie hide her notes from their lessons. She promised she'd put them in their safe so even their kids couldn't stumble upon them.

Then, he suggested they begin working on alternate personas they might adopt, in case anyone showed too much interest in their relationship with him. "With strangers, or even your customers, you may need to pull on a crazy persona, as I do, to keep people from figuring you out. Believe me, no one will take you seriously if you act like a maniac... should the need arise.

"Likely, no one will come to question you about time travel. You won't be as blatant as I am, out giving lectures on time travel ethics. My Grampa worked as a psychiatrist to keep a low profile. As news people, any digging or questioning you do will seem like business as usual, and I believe it will keep you under the radar. Who would guess a reporter, or a photographer, is a time traveler?"

Mig said, "We don't plan on publishing any of this. Don't worry."

"That doesn't seem safe," said Carrie.

Peter agreed. "Well, as long as you don't publish stories with details you couldn't possibly know, or quote conversations you could not have heard, no one will suspect you are anything more than inquisitive journalists."

"So, who are you going to be?" Mig asked.

Carrie, in the passenger seat, turned sideways to face Mig as he drove them home. From the smirk on his face, she guessed that he'd already chosen the persona he wanted to put on when discretion called for it.

That wasn't foremost in her mind, however. "Shouldn't we talk about you sparking up the room? You started to time travel, Mig."

"I don't wanna talk about that right now," he said. Carrie saw his features tense, his face changed from the smirk of a moment ago to grim as he stared through the windshield.

"Okay, I totally understand. Let's leave it for another time," she said.

He hit the turn signal and glanced at her, a forced smile on his face, before returning his gaze to the road.

Carrie dropped it and followed up on his question about what persona to adopt when needed. "Okay, who are you going to be?"

"Don Quixote de La Mancha," Mig said, his face lighting up with a wide grin.

Carrie rolled her eyes, turning away so Mig didn't see her do it. "I don't think that's exactly what Peter meant, but okay." She drew out the *okay* for several seconds.

"What? It's perfect," Mig looked at her briefly then went back to watching the road. He turned as they approached their neighborhood, passing a farmer chugging home on a tractor. "Listen. Don Quixote is already a guy who has trouble getting anyone to take him seriously. I'll just act like him, if it becomes necessary. I mean, we write strange news, but we don't run around talking about time travel like Peter does. We're under the radar. He's right about that."

"True," Carrie said. "So, you'll be *Miguel de Cervantes* instead of *Miguel Weathers*. Okay." Carrie shook her head, secretly looking forward to seeing her husband in character.

When the Weathers arrived home, Mig poured two glasses of sun tea and slid one across the kitchen counter to Carrie. Settling onto the living room couch, Mig switched on the television, tuning to the 6 o'clock weekend news.

Carrie heated leftovers for dinner — not Mig's favorite, but she didn't have the energy left to cook — and they ate in silence, each lost in their own thoughts and barely listening to the TV.

When they finished eating, Carrie took her plate to the kitchen — grabbing Mig's empty plate on the way. "Do you want more?" she asked.

"Maybe in a little while," Mig said, distractedly. Carrie set their plates on the counter, covered the remaining food with plastic wrap, and returned to her seat next to him in the living room, placing two freshened iced teas on the table.

"Do you want to talk about the lesson today? What happened to you?" Carrie saw him tense up again, before blowing out a long breath.

"I felt it. You know? I felt myself approaching the restaurant. I could tell it wasn't *today*, either. Not sure how to explain it, but it's almost like I could feel the days winding backward to our lunch.

"And it all happened in an instant." He shook his head. "This is powerful stuff, Carrie. I'm excited, exhilarated, even. But it's powerful. Kinda freaking me out a little, and I need to get my head wrapped around it. Can we leave it for now?"

She gripped his hand in hers. "Sure. I want to know more, not just because I'm curious but because I can't do it. I'm pretty sure at this point, since I don't feel anything. Just... I want to understand how it feels for you."

"I know," he said. He kissed her, squeezed her hand, then released it and turned up the TV volume.

Okay, distraction it is, Carrie thought. With the news program scheduled to end soon, Carrie asked if he'd like to watch a movie. She then realized he was turning up the TV's volume again. She was about to protest, when he leaned forward in his seat, watching with sudden interest.

The news anchor was describing a robbery. An intruder attacked the woman and got away with the family's cash, computer, and television. She was in the hospital. Her two children had been in the house and, thankfully, were unharmed, having slept through it all. The identity of the attacker was unknown, the woman telling police it was someone she'd never seen before, and police were investigating.

"That's not far from here," Mig said. He tilted his head and looked at Carrie.

She saw the look in his eyes and knew instantly what he was thinking. "You're thinking you and Peter might save her," she said, looking down to prevent Mig from seeing the fear rising in her eyes.

"Me, and Peter, and *you*," he said. "Maybe. But think about it. This is what we've been talking about. What if what happened to this family can be changed?" Mig looked back at the TV. The anchor had already moved on to another story. "Corrections, wife."

Goosebumps rose on Carrie's arms as she realized: now that they knew about time travel, it would affect everything. All the time.

She hesitated, watching her iced tea shaking as her hands trembled, then said, "Go for it, sweetheart," and steeled herself for what was to come.

Mig picked up his smart phone and dialed Peter. Carrie listened as Mig filled Peter in, and they arranged to meet the following evening, the 12th of October to formulate a travel plan.

Peter ended the phone call.

He had agreed to meet them, and to take a trip related to a robbery that had just happened near Mig and Carrie's home. *It seems like a simple enough correction*, Peter thought, *which is a good place to start with them.*

For him, it was an opportunity to find out how they'd do under pressure. More importantly, it was a chance to test Mig's budding time travel ability.

The sooner the Weathers were acclimated, the better. He was eager to get them helping so he could save Silvia... and Valerie.

10 – Relativity

Soon after ending his call with Mig, Peter heard a knock on his door. Looking at the clock, he saw it was 6:30 P.M., and wondered who it could be. Not the Weathers, certainly, as he'd just hung up with them.

He answered his door and was greeted by a mustachioed man in an expensive-looking suit, leaning on a cane. Peter returned the greeting, pulling on his maniacal persona just in case, then looking the man over carefully. Something seemed familiar about him.

"I'm Roman Vasquez," the man said. "I'm looking for Alfonso Horacio. I'm his cousin." The man spoke in a soft, lilting voice, which to Peter sounded exaggeratedly friendly.

"Roman?" Peter looked at him in surprise, then extended his hand. He hadn't known his grandfather had any cousins — at least, he didn't remember him mentioning any, nonetheless one name Roman. "Nice to meet you, cousin Roman. I'm Peter, and Alfonso is my grandfather. I'm sorry, but he's no longer with us."

Roman pouted his lips, "I'm sorry to hear." His voice rising again, he asked, "Did he tell you of me?"

"I'm sorry, no." Peter wouldn't have told the stranger anyway if he had.

"Well, your grandfather was, as I am, descended from the original sojourners, as my father referred to our ancestors. I am happy to meet you, as it's been a long time since I've seen any of our relatives. I had thought I was the last one standing in the world, cousin."

Peter pricked up his ears at the odd phrasing, since the man had asked for Alfonso when Peter opened the door. Why was the man here if he didn't think Alfonso was alive? And why hadn't he asked what happened to his grandfather? People always ask what happened. Peter made a mental note to reach out to his Grampa — who was not dead-gone but living-in-the-future-gone — and ask about this mysterious *cousin.*

"I am a time traveler, like Alfonso, and like you," Roman said, peering closely at Peter. "I saw an article about you online. I recognized the photograph for what it was — not a ghost, as the article read, but as the boundary around a time traveler's safe area. *Your* safe area."

Peter adopted a confused expression. "I don't know what you mean. Are you well, Roman?" Peter exaggerated his movements, acting as oddly as he could. "I'm a speaker on ethics of time travel, but certainly such a thing isn't possible yet."

Roman glared at him. The older man's expression gave Peter pause. Something did not feel right. "I'm sorry we've not met before, Roman. Why have you come here to see my grandfather, after so many years?" Peter asked.

Roman didn't respond to the question. Instead, he told Peter that he was glad to know there was another time traveler, ignoring Peter's denials. "May I come in?"

Leading Roman into his kitchen. Peter figured it was best to keep his crazy persona going until he could find out more about this person purporting to be family, but fully a stranger to him.

He offered coffee, but Roman declined, asking for water. Peter filled a glass and placed it in front of the older man. "What brings you here, Roman?"

Instead of answering Peter's question, Roman launched into their family's history. "Likely you know from your grandfather that we can trace our roots back to the great-grandfathers settling, in 1838, in what is now New Mexico. There were three brothers," Roman paused in thought. "Well, four, but the fourth died soon after they settled in New Mexico. Three brothers carried on. They took the name Horacio from a neighbor, a man who died not long after they met him. Over time, each of the three brothers married and raised families. My great-grandfather married a native woman. He changed our name to Vasquez around that time."

Roman paused, as if thinking of something he might add, then shook his head before continuing. "Anyway, the two other brothers got married, too: one to a local woman — a Latina as they say now — and the other to a woman I don't remember anything about. Maybe my father never told me." He waved his hand dismissively. "She doesn't matter. Anyway, between the three of them, the brothers had nine children, though only four or so survived to adulthood. One of those children was my grandfather, another was your great-great-grandfather, I believe." The older man shrugged.

This was more than Peter's Grampa had shared with him about the family. Peter felt gaps filling in as Roman spoke.

"I am here to ask for your help," Roman said, finally getting around to answering Peter's question. "I have lost my children, and I am in need of help."

"I'm sorry for your loss," Peter said, "but, what help could I give?"

"You don't understand, cousin," Roman sighed. "I traveled back in time. I remember going back to save my children, and others who were harmed that day. Yet, my children are gone again. I believe someone else has traveled back and changed the timeline after me."

Peter understood that Roman was insinuating there was yet another time traveler who, for whatever reason, was intentionally thwarting Roman. Again, it didn't jibe with Roman's comment that he thought he was the only time traveler alive.

Peter thought carefully before responding. "So, if, for the moment, I assume you believe a time traveler is involved," Peter flourished his hands widely, adopting a skeptical expression, "how do you believe my knowledge of time travel ethics could be of help? Certainly, I don't really travel through time, so I hope you don't suspect me of harming your children. Even if time travel were possible, I would never do such a cruel thing."

Roman's eyes narrowed. Peter continued. "Tell me what you remember changing, what you believe has changed back, and what you think a time traveler — another time traveler — has done to you."

Roman blew out a great sigh and leaned back in his chair. Instead of challenging Peter, Roman talked for over an hour. Peter took notes, catching every detail he could and drawing a timeline with milestones for each version of events that Roman believed he'd experienced. He took care to ensure Roman could not see his notes.

As he spoke, Roman pulled out a packet of photographs. He placed them on the counter, one by one, naming the people in the photographs. One photograph Roman slid across to Peter. "Here, this one you keep."

It was a photograph of Peter's grandfather with another man. Roman pointed at his grandfather in the photo. "You know this is Alfonso. The taller man is Alfonso's father, Manuel. It is better you have this as it is of your family and not mine."

Again, Peter thought the man's phrasing odd. *Why would he refer to his cousin, and uncle, as not his family?*

Roman paused to sip at his water. Peter seized the moment to take a good look at the old man. Roman was close to his Grampa's age, but much more careworn. When Grampa had approached the age of 100, his hair had turned slowly to salt-and-pepper, a few wrinkles forming around his eyes. Roman's hair was mostly gray, his eyes surrounded by wrinkles as thick as folds, and his cheeks were sunken. Peter imagined that

Roman must have lived a hard life and it showed, despite the wellspring of youth time traveling had offered.

When the older man set down his water glass, picked up his cane and slowly pulled himself upright. He clutched the cane in both hands and fixed an unsettling stare on Peter. "You continue your deception if you must, but I know what you are. I'm staying in the area for some time, now. I'll give you a few days to think, and then I'll come see you again."

After Roman left, Peter decided he needed information only his grandfather could give him, to determine if Roman was telling the truth. Peter believed Roman was going to come back. His mind went to Mig and Carrie, who would be coming over tomorrow night for a trip to stop the robbery in their neck of the woods. He shook this problem from his head, refocusing himself on his immediate need: to reach out to his grandfather. *I'll worry about our trip tomorrow*, he told himself. *What I need to do right now is ask Grampa about Roman.*

Sitting down at his desk, Peter took several deep breaths, then picked up a pen. He thought long and hard about what to include in a newspaper classified ad — his special way of reaching his Grampa, who had gone forward years ago and lived in the future. His grandfather had called it, "A time traveler's retirement." Still, in their own ways, they stayed in touch.

Carefully Peter crafted the wording. The ad read:

Grampa: Happy Birthday! Join your family at Roman's restaurant. Love, P.H.

The 'Happy Birthday' he included in most of his messages as a way for the message to blend in with other classifieds. In addition, each year on his Grampa's birthday,

Peter placed a classified ad that simply read, 'Happy Birthday, Love, P.H.' Grampa always called him P.H., never using Peter's last initial, despising Peter's father as he did.

Even when Grampa didn't reach out in response, it made Peter feel more connected to him.

Rereading the ad text, Peter wasn't sure that the brief mention of Roman would get the job done, especially since Grampa might not know Roman. It might all be a ruse. *Do I believe Roman is family?* Peter wondered. He thought of when he'd first opened his front door and the man had seemed familiar. There was a chance Roman was telling the truth about being family. He revised the message to read:

Grampa: Happy Birthday! Come celebrate with me at Cousin Roman's family restaurant. Food is like yours from New Mexico now in North Carolina. Love, P.H.

Good enough, Peter thought, and navigated to the Denver newspaper website to place the classified ad. He hoped Grampa would respond soon. *If he's still looking for my ads in the newspaper. Even a time traveler must run out of time eventually, right?*

There was no one to answer Peter's question.

11 – Distraction

The morning of October 12th, as soon as the Weathers stepped inside, Peter shut the front door. Rather than walking to the kitchen, he leaned against the door, as if holding back a horde, and said, "I know we need to go over what you've found out about the home invasion. First, I have something to tell you. It's good, perhaps, or bad, maybe, but odd either way."

Carrie stared at him, waiting for the odd man to explain what he had found to be odd.

"Coffee first," Mig said, as he handed Peter a steaming to-go cup.

"Thank you," Peter said, absentmindedly taking the cup from Mig's hand. "I've had another time traveler show up at my door."

Carrie, who had taken a drink of her coffee, just managed to get her hand up before choking and spraying coffee from her mouth. Her hand blocked it from hitting the men. Peter pulled tissues from a box on a nearby table and handed them to her.

Mig took a long drink of his coffee, watching Peter over the cup's rim. "Okay," he said, drawing out the word.

Carrie wiped the floor and backed into the kitchen. She cleaned herself up, then sat down on one of the tall chairs, taking a small, careful sip.

Slowly, the men followed her into the kitchen, Peter speaking in a voice she thought matched the one used by his crazy persona. Except this time, she didn't think he was acting.

"It's unbelievable. The only time travelers I knew of were my mother and Grampa — and he didn't speak much of family. As far as I knew, Grampa was the first time traveler. Well, and my mother was, but she stopped traveling years before I was born. I knew no one else who was kin except Grandma. This seems unbelievable." His voice stayed at a high pitch throughout his diatribe.

"How do you know he's for real?" Mig asked. "This guy could be lying."

Peter shook his head as he sat, almost missing the tall chair in the process. He straightened himself onto its seat. "I don't. And I didn't let on anything of my own abilities, although the description he gave of his own abilities matched, and he knew quite a bit about my family. He had family photos, too," Peter said, pointing to a black-and-white photograph on the counter.

"Did he say how he found you? Maybe he visited this house when it was your grandfather's. Is that possible?" Carrie asked.

Peter shrugged exaggeratedly, both arms flailing up and dropping.

He started at the beginning, telling Mig and Carrie about his visitor's arrival, Roman's sharing of family details, and flailing his arms again as he explained why Roman said he had come. "He's asked for my help, and I'm not sure whether I should give it."

Peter sighed, and under his breath said, "I won't know that without hearing from Grampa."

"Your Grampa? How--" Carrie started to ask, but Peter cut her off.

"We can talk about him another time, and Roman, too. Let's get on with your training. The sooner you grasp the basics, the better." He stood and drained his coffee cup, tapping the end to get the last drop.

He practically bounded down the stairs to his office, Carrie watched, open-mouthed, then slowly rose. Mig mouthed,

Wow to Carrie before following Peter down the stairs, Carrie bringing up the rear.

As they entered Peter's office, he stopped suddenly and snatched a piece of paper from his desk.

"What's the matter?" Mig asked.

Peter looked at the paper, then grabbed reading glasses from the desk and slid them on. "It's from my Grampa."

Mig walked around the desk and looked at the note. "I thought you said your Grampa was dead."

"Not dead. He's gone, living in the future," Peter responded. "I sent him a note, and am glad he's already responded. This will either allay my fears or confirm my gut feeling not to trust Roman." The note read:

Hello P.H.:

Cousin Roman is not to my taste. Be wary.

Think. Why would Roman come to you? Perhaps he knows somehow that I'm gone. Don't let him use you. Whatever he says, assume it's not the whole truth.

He may think he's older and wiser, but you are wise, and you have experience. I'm confident you will outsmart him.

Of New Mexico, you must know now that I was born in a special place there. I should have taken you. I'm sorry I kept you away, but your mother and I thought separation was for the best. We adopted North Carolina as our home, your home.

Here is a map. I hope you will go and see this place on

my birth day in 1898. I would like you to be there. It is a place when you can learn much. Adell can be trusted.

Roman and his self-named Vasquez kin can not.

Love, Grampa

Peter's eyes teared up as he finished reading. He sat down in his desk chair with a thump. "Why didn't you wake me, Grampa?" Peter said aloud. He clutched at the note. "I'm glad to have a reply, and to know I'm right not to trust Roman."

Carrie watched as Peter dropped the paper onto his desk and traced his finger over the map at the bottom of the paper. Unsure what to do as she saw Peter's eyes watering, she sat down as quietly as she could in one of the desk-front chairs, averting her eyes.

Mig sat down in the other chair facing Peter's desk.

After a moment, seeming to remember he wasn't alone, Peter wiped his eyes, then looked at Mig. "Family secrets. Why do families keep secrets from each other? Especially when there are so many things we did share." He sighed.

"Family is complicated," Mig said.

Peter looked at him, nodding as he blew out a breath, "Yeah, I know."

Peter had been raised mostly by his mother, who was intelligent and kind to him, while his father paid no attention. His father had been loud and standoffish, a heavy drinker who'd thought of himself and never of his wife or young sons. He'd died during World War II while Peter was still a boy.

That's when Peter's Grampa had stepped in, taking Peter and Peter's brother, Simon, under his wing, and helping their mother, Grampa's daughter Renee, stay afloat. They'd all moved into the big house his grandfather owned in Hope Wells, and happier times had come, at least for a while.

Peter knew his mother had been a time traveler, although she had stopped traveling when she became pregnant with Simon. She'd aged normally all of Peter's life, and she'd never involved herself in Peter's lessons, or his and his grandfather's travels.

When Peter's brother Simon had died — killed on a sidewalk by a drunk driver in a fast-moving Chevy — finding out from his grandfather that they were time travelers had seemed a blessing to Peter.

It had been his first hard life lesson, too, and with his grandfather's guidance, including discussions on the obligations of time travelers not to abuse their power for themselves. Grampa had led Peter to the decision to let his brother go. It had been hard for Peter; sometimes since he had wondered if, had he not been new to time travel, he might have made a different decision. It helped that his grandfather always said it was the right decision to let a time traveler go to rest, and stay there.

Learning that there was a secret place his grandfather and mother had kept from him, on top of the strange visit from Roman, and the tutoring of his apprentices, Peter felt the weight of the world. He sighed heavily, then looked up at the Weathers and forced other thoughts out of his head. *Focus on today, on now,* he thought as he pushed the note away.

Carrie saw a change in Peter as he set the note aside. His eyes brightened, and she could almost hear his brain switching gears as he turned his attention on them.

He leaned forward in his desk chair, causing it to squeak. Flipping open a notebook and picking up a pen, he said, "If you want to help this woman, then we will. It will be good experience, and move your knowledge forward, and I'll be glad to have you both up-to-speed. So, tell me why you want to save this woman in particular."

Carrie, unsure what criteria Peter was looking for, offered, "Well, she has two kids. I mean," she cleared her throat. "Her name is Mrs. Brenda Walters, and she has two young children, and a husband. What is a good enough reason to help her?"

Peter wrote for a moment. "What do you think?"

Carrie shrugged. She looked at Mig, hopeful he would respond.

Mig leaned forward, elbows on Peter's desk. "We don't know her, but she doesn't live far from us, and she's been put in the hospital. Plus, she has a family, as Carrie said. You tell us, Peter. What makes a person worth helping?"

Peter sat quietly, appearing to review the notes he'd written as the two of them were speaking. He leaned back in his chair, bringing about another squeak, and said, "If you believe this is a worthy cause, why would I stop you? Would helping her break any of my rules?"

"No," Mig and Carrie said together.

Peter scribbled again. "Okay, then, how do we use time travel to help this Mrs. Walters and her family?" He'd used his professorial tone, and stared at the two of them.

"Ah, a teachable moment?" Carrie said. "Let the amateurs hone their planning skills, right?"

When Peter nodded, Mig said, "I'm up for it. I think we start with the home invasion. We stop the attacker from getting into her house."

"But how do you stop them without you and Peter getting hurt?" Carrie asked. It came out at a higher pitch than she had intended.

"It's okay," Peter said, motioning slow-down with his open hand. "Let's get to details, and as we create a plan, we will be mindful of keeping ourselves safe, too."

"Why not call the police before it happens?" Carrie asked? "Path of least resistance..."

Peter nodded profusely. His reading glasses bounced on his nose, and he removed them. "You'd be surprised how often a simple plan is the best plan," Peter said, still nodding. "Let's start there. Okay, so let's say we arrive early at the location, watch for anyone to skulk toward the house, and call the police immediately before they get inside. Did the woman--"

"Mrs. Walters," Carrie offered.

Peter continued, "Did Mrs. Walters give any description to the police? What did you find out so far?"

"Nothing. According to what I found online, including the police report, she said it was one man, and she gave no description. She said it was dark in the house, as she was about to go to bed. Her children were already in bed, so they didn't see anything." Carrie said.

Mig offered, "What if the po-po don't get there quick enough?"

Peter chuckled at Mig's use of the term *po-po*, then thought for a moment. "Well, if the police don't arrive quickly enough, I guess we'd need to make some noise to scare the intruder away, and hope the police catch him before he gets far. Even if he isn't caught, the woman will be safe. That's the priority."

"True. Okay." Mig said.

Carrie raised a finger, then lowered it. "Um, making noise... What if his guy comes after you? Or, um, us?" The *us* came out as a whisper, and she saw one of Peter's eyebrows rise.

Turning to Mig, Peter said, "Tell me what you think about that."

"Well," Mig said, "I don't want somebody coming after any of us. So, I guess... our safety will depend on making the *right* noises. Robbers would run away if they thought they were about to get caught, right? So, we just need to make it sound like there's people coming."

Carrie suggested, "Why not put the sound of a police siren on your phone, Mig? You can play it if the police aren't coming fast enough."

"Sure!" Mig agreed, typing quickly on his smart phone. "I'll add a couple options to my play-list, and we'll use them if we have to."

"If we have to," Peter stressed, looking at Carrie. He raised his eyebrow again, and she blushed. She felt as if he was looking inside her, seeing her anxiety. Forcing a smile, she saw both of Peter's eyebrows go up.

She told herself it was going to be all right, that they were making a safe plan. "Okay with me."

Peter dropped his gaze to his notebook. "Carrie, what time did the robbery happen?" Peter's pen hovered over the page.

Carrie unlocked her phone, and after a moment found what she wanted online. She read aloud, "Police responded after a call from the husband, Mark Walters, who arrived home at 8 P.M. He told police he had found his wife in the kitchen, beaten, and his children asleep, the back door unlocked, and she told police she was going to bed and had the lights out." Carrie frowned. "It happened before her husband got home. She was going to bed pretty early."

"Could be what's normal for her, what with two young kids. I mean, not everyone is a night owl," Peter offered.

"It gets dark around 5 o'clock or thereabouts. Can we assume the bad guy arrived after dark?" Mig offered.

Peter pulled his laptop toward him and brought up a Google map showing the Walters' address. He pointed to a copse of trees. "Best to be safe and arrive during daylight and wait. I think we can hide ourselves in this area." He pointed at the map on his screen.

Carrie raised her hand as if a child in a class — she realized Peter had been speaking in his professorial mode again — then lowered it. "I'd prefer not to go on this trip, if that's okay. Or if you need me, to keep yourselves safer, I can. But, how many of us does it take to call the police? I mean, three people, even two people, when one could..." She trailed off, blushing, then added, "I'm being selfish, but..." and grew silent.

"I don't think we all need to go," Mig said, and Carrie brightened. "But I'd like to go with Peter." Carrie drooped.

Peter held up his hand and tapped the air with it in the *slow down* motion Carrie had noticed he used frequently. "I'm happy to go alone. I'm happy to have one or both of you come along. The goal is to save this woman from being beaten. Well, my personal goal, if I may be frank, is to ensure the two of you learn from me. This is an opportunity, from my point of view, to take a trip during which you can gain experience." He looked at Carrie, "It's not as scary as you're imagining it to be. The sooner you take a trip, the faster you'll see that."

12 – Poof

Mig and Peter chose to go back in time, and Carrie elected to stay in the time travel room.

As the men prepared to travel, Peter handed Carrie a few of his files to read. "Consider this your homework since you're not traveling with us. As always, don't leave the room," he reminded.

She wondered how many times Peter was going to repeat himself, then realized how few lessons they'd actually had, compared to the power of what they were learning. *Better to hear it a million times than forget*, she thought. *This isn't cooking lessons where mistakes can be eaten.* Her greatest fear was that she'd make a mistake.

"Be careful," she said. She pushed a pillow behind her back, leaning against the rear wall of the time travel room. Minutes after they'd gone, the sweet scent increased, enveloped her, and she drifted off to a dreamless sleep.

Peter and Mig disappeared from the time travel room, and arrived the afternoon of October 11th, behind the small house where the home invasion had taken place.

"I feel normal," Mig said. "I don't know what I expected, but this feels like I'd feel if I were walking around your yard with you on a normal day."

"Normal is good," Peter said, his eyes scanning the area.

After a moment, Mig added, "Actually, I feel mostly normal. Somehow, I also know this is not my time. Is that how it is for you?"

"Yes," Peter said, beginning to move toward the woods. Mig followed stealthily. "I can tell where and when I am, and that I'm still connected back to my time. Our time."

They moved inside the woods nearby. Once he'd found a spot where they could see the house but not be seen, Peter stopped and motioned for Mig to get down. They waited for the invader to arrive.

The men were shocked to discover that things were not as expected. The two travelers watched as the woman pulled laundry from a line, the children playing nearby under a tall street lamp. Across the lawn, they watched as a woman with lanky, slick blonde hair emerged from the trailer home next door. She was followed by a scruffy-looking man in a US flag t-shirt and ripped jeans. The disheveled couple walked across the lawn toward Mrs. Walters.

Seeing them, Mrs. Walters dropped the clothing in her hand and said something to the blonde woman.

Suddenly, the blonde pushed Mrs. Walters to the ground. In a loud voice, the woman from the trailer said, "We need money. You go get it now."

Mrs. Walters said something back to her that they couldn't hear, then yelled for her children to run into the house.

The scruffy man grabbed the little girl as she ran. He squeezed the girl's back to his chest and yelled, "Go get us money now!"

Mrs. Walters scrambled up and ran to her back door, pushing her son in ahead of her. She emerged almost immediately waving cash in her hand. "This is all of it. I'll give you all of it. Please let go of my girl."

"I'm gonna check the house for stuff we can sell," the blonde woman said as her companion gripped the little girl. She cried, saying "Mama," over and over between sobs.

Peter said, "This is it. We need to stop this now."

Mig pulled out his cell phone to call the police. Before he could type 9-1-1, Peter put his hand over Mig's phone. "Don't call. I know that's what we planned, but there's no time."

"Okay. What do we do?"

"New plan." Without warning, Peter jumped up from behind their cover of bushes and ran toward the group.

Peter ran directly into the man, grabbing at his free arm, as Mig ran up and scooped the little girl away.

Peter shoved the man to the ground, then he turned to face the greasy-haired woman.

Mig handed the girl to her mother and said firmly, "Get inside." He moved beside Peter, his eyes fixed on the man on the ground.

The young woman backed up, wiping her nose with her palm. Peter reached out and snatched the cash from her other hand. "Let's go," she said to her mate. She turned and ran back to her trailer next door, the man followed in a shambling, crouched run.

"So, what the heck?" Peter said, his eyes on the trailer with the two failed thieves inside.

"You want my guess, I'd say Mrs. Walters lied because the people who put her in the hospital live right there. She's probably scared of them. Scared for her kids, too, which is probably why she told the police the kids were in bed. Keep them from being questioned."

"She lied. I get it," Peter said. "Well, we better smarten her up right now."

Peter knocked on the Walters' screen door. The woman squealed, "Go away." The sounds of children crying drifted out to them.

Peter faced her through the screen and held up his hands. "We're not going to hurt you. We saw them coming and just wanted to help. Please don't be afraid."

She responded with a whimper that rose at the end, almost like a question.

Peter took a step backward. "Ma'am..." Peter looked toward Mig and mouthed *Name?*

"Walters," Mig said.

"Mrs. Walters. You need to call 9-1-1. If you don't report your neighbors, they are just going to do this to you again."

The woman's eyes had grown wider, and she'd begun shaking. Peter continued in a more forceful tone, "Think about your kids. Call 9-1-1, or get your kids in the car and go straight to the sheriff's office. All right?"

"They're not going to stop just because you don't report them," Mig added.

Finally, she nodded, then pulled out her cell phone. She tried and failed to dial, starting over twice before dropping her phone.

Peter stepped forward, opened the screen, and picked up the phone. Mrs. Walters stared at him, her eyes wide, but didn't retreat.

When did he put gloves on? Mig wondered. *The old man sure is prepared.*

Peter dialed 9-1-1 and handed the cell phone back to her. She pressed Send and held the phone to her ear.

Peter turned and led Mig away until he was sure they were out of the woman's sight. "Let's go."

The two travelers closed their eyes, drew in deep breaths, and disappeared together in a cloud of black, returning to their own time.

When Mig woke up the next morning, he grabbed his tablet and surfed to the county sheriff's website. After a few minutes of digging, he found the incident. There were few details, except notations that two arrests had been made.

Mig nudged Carrie awake and showed her his tablet's screen. "Carrie, you're not gonna believe what really happened last night.... er, on... on our trip to October 11th." He rubbed his eyes hard, as if waking from an unbelievable dream.

Carrie sat up. "Tell me," she said, suddenly wide awake.

Mig told her the whole story of he and Peter's trip the night before, ending with, "We fixed the problem, though not as we'd planned."

"Mrs. Walters isn't in the hospital. That's better than before," Carrie said, adding, "That poor woman, being stuck next door to those awful people." She shook her head.

Mig leaned over and kissed her. "Well, thanks to time travel, she didn't get hurt. She reported them, too, so maybe the neighbors will go to jail, and the Walters family can have some peace."

"Thanks to you and crazy old Peter," she said, ruffling his goatee with her fingers. "This is all so incredible."

"Come next time, okay?"

Carrie had just climbed out of bed, her back to Mig. She turned toward him. "I'm afraid I'll mess something up, or get you guys hurt."

"Peter and I will do the traveling. Well, mostly Peter. All you have to do is ride along. I promise you, it feels amazing to move through time."

Carrie hugged him. "Promise I can't break anything, and I'll go."

13 – The Missing Student

The week before Halloween, Mig and Carrie grew busy with what Carrie had begun referring to as "their real jobs" — consciously devoting most weekdays to the newspaper now that time travel was taking up Saturdays and many of their conversations. Carrie had many articles to complete. Plus, Mig had customers to visit, ensuring upcoming Black Friday sales started being advertised now.

It was early on Friday, the day before their next lesson, when Mig received a phone call from Peter. He switched the call to speaker.

"Something's come up. I know we just returned from helping Mrs. Walters, and I've got things I'd prefer to work on, but I have something that's been brought to my attention. We can set a plan, and you and Carrie can come with me to make a correction."

Mig explained to Peter that Carrie had articles to finish, and he had meetings in another town, but he'd be home by dinnertime. He told Peter he was welcome to come by their house around 5 P.M. if it couldn't wait until Saturday.

Carrie overheard him giving Peter directions, and she jumped up and began straightening the house.

Mig ended the call. "The house is fine, sweetheart," he said to Carrie as she hurried around. "You just cleaned it Wednesday so the kids would see it clean on Thursday, and you cleaned it again last night after they left. Well, *we* cleaned it after they left," he jibed playfully. She laughed and continued straightening, tossing miscellaneous objects in drawers.

When both Mig and Peter arrived promptly at 5 o'clock, Carrie surprised them with an early dinner waiting on the table.

As they ate, Peter got down to business. "I ran into a woman I know yesterday at the grocery store. She's a professor; Margaret Bonner's her name. She came to a presentation of mine years ago, and once invited me to speak to the ethics class she teaches at the college. Anyway, we got to talking, and she seemed upset. I asked her what was going on. Then, the floodgates opened, if you know what I mean."

Margaret had poured out to Peter that one of her students was a missing person. "Margaret's very worried. She'd seen her student arguing with a young man in the college parking lot, but they drove away before Margaret reached the car. She meant to intervene and ensure her student," Peter flipped open a notebook, "whose name is Clara Day, was all right. Clara has not been seen since, and she missed her next class that day, according to another professor Margaret knows. I believe Clara went missing Wednesday after Margaret's 8:30 A.M. class ended."

"A missing person?" Mig frowned, then asked, "Missing like the police are involved, or like she didn't show up for class and the teacher is worried?"

Peter explained that Margaret had already talked with the police, telling them everything she could remember about the man Clara was arguing with and his car. "That was yesterday, after Clara's parents had officially reported her missing. Margaret is afraid something bad has happened. I think she's feeling guilty about not reaching the car in time. From what Margaret has told me, the young man she saw arguing with Clara was driving an older, beat-up car, maybe a classic, and Clara drove away with him. None of Clara's family have heard from her for two days now, and she's posted nothing on social media," Peter checked his notes. "Margaret spoke with several of Clara's classmates, who say that's unusual. Her online silence doesn't bode well."

"Have the police found the man?" Carrie asked.

"Not as of this afternoon, they haven't. I checked in with a contact at the department — it's the Wilson Police Department — and nothing so far. Margaret doesn't know cars, so they're having trouble coming up with a make and model. Nothing on the security cameras at the college, either."

Carrie clutched Mig's hand and squeezed. He squeezed back, then asked, "What's the plan, Peter?"

"That's why I'm here. A plan needs to be devised." Peter stood. He began to pace and folded his hands together, tapping his fingertips against his chin. After a few moments of pacing, he stopped and asked them, "If there's no way of knowing where she is now or what's happened, then doesn't it make the most sense to focus on where she *was*?"

"In the school parking lot?" Mig asked.

"Yes," Peter confirmed as he began pacing again, "Or before she reaches it. She'd just left Margaret's class a short time before Margaret saw her in the car. So, we should be able to intercept Clara at the classroom."

"There's something else we need to consider," Carrie interrupted. "If Clara knows this man, or has a relationship with him, stopping her from getting in the car with him, on that day, may be a temporary fix. He may just hurt her — or whatever he might have done — on a future date."

She looked at Mig, then at Peter, neither of them responded. Both seemed to be thinking hard.

Finally, Peter said. "One day at a time, Carrie. We do what we can. I've dealt with abuse problems before. It can take a little more time, and it might require more than one trip. We can start with the *who*, *where*, and *when* that we have to solve Clara's immediate problem. Margaret's, too."

Carrie thought she saw a dark expression pass across Peter's face, then it was gone. "What's wrong?"

Peter's thoughts had flooded with the names of the murdered women, these others waiting for him to help them, for him to begin setting a plan with the Weathers.

Now is not the time to worry about them, he told himself, and shook his head to clear it. "Nothing is wrong. Just a lot going on right now. We'll focus on Margaret, and let other things wait," he said, ignoring Carrie's questioning look.

"What else do we need to know to help you with Margaret?" Mig asked.

"For sure we need to know what time the class ends, and what Clara looks like," Carrie said.

"Oh, darn it, yes," Peter said. "I need to get a photo from Margaret. When we go back to intercept Clara, the Margaret from then isn't going to know why I'm there, so I won't be able to ask her to point Clara out. She'd probably think I was being creepy."

"Not necessarily. You spoke to her class," Carrie reminded Peter. "Stopping by to talk with one of her students shouldn't be a big deal."

"Still, having a photo before we travel back will make it easier," Mig suggested.

"Fewer questions to ask when we get there," Peter agreed, nodding. "Good idea, Carrie."

Peter filed through the notes he'd made when speaking with Margaret. He and Mig went over them; Mig asking questions, and Peter trying to fill in blanks so they could plan for their trip.

Carrie grabbed a cup of coffee and sat down on the living room couch. While they came up with ideas for changing events in the parking lot where Clara disappeared, Carrie picked up her laptop and searched on social media until she found

Clara Day, a current student at the community college where Peter's friend Margaret taught. "Here's a few photos, maybe, if I have the right Clara Day."

Peter and Mig looked over from the dining room. Carrie swiveled the laptop screen toward them. Peter approached for a closer look.

"Okay, right school, right name. Before we travel, I'll double check with Margaret to be sure."

"Wait a minute! I forgot," Carrie said, typing into the search bar. "With police involved there should be a missing person notice. Ugh, I'm an idiot. Here, found it." She turned the laptop again, showing Mig and Peter.

Mig stood and came closer. "Okay, that's definitely her. We're good, then." Mig said, as he headed for the coffee pot.

Carrie asked Peter, "When do we need to leave our time to intercept Clara back on the day she disappeared?"

Mig asked, "Does it matter *when* we leave? There's not a limit on how many days we can go backwards, is there, Peter?"

Peter wavered his hand in a *maybe-yes, maybe-no* gesture. He said, "Not really, Mig. I don't like to wait too long if I can help it. Depends on how long it takes to come up with a *good* plan. As to the day, no, there isn't a limit, and we can go backward from any day, so that's flexible. Except... the more time passes, the more Clara's family and others related to this event will continue on with their lives. The more days we wait, the more things will happen in their lives that we'll delete when we change the timeline by keeping Clara from being abducted. As to the time, I'll check with Margaret what time she ended the class. As to when we should leave our time, I think you two should come over late even though you won't be sleeping in the time travel room."

Peter sighed as he thought again of Silvia Andrews and Valerie Edmonds. Dead, and — as he thought of it — waiting for him to come up with a way to save them. He knew he wasn't ready though. He'd managed to get the help he needed, but wasn't going to broach the subject of the serial killer with his new apprentices yet. Saving Mrs. Walters had been quick, and Clara's situation looked like it might be, compared to hunting, identifying, and stopping the serial killer. He forced himself to focus on their planning for the immediate problem — Clara's plight.

Mig was pacing now. "Okay. We know what Clara looks like. We can intercept her at class. How do we get rid of the man in the car?"

"That's a good question, and a part of the plan where things will be uncertain. We don't know who he is, or what he's done, so we need to be cautious but firm. We need to get him to leave the parking lot."

"Or taken away," Carrie said. "It's on campus so there's probably campus security. How about getting them involved?"

Mig bit his lip. "More police. Peter, are you telling me you never had a problem of existing while brown?"

"I have, Mig. I get it. But Carrie's point is valid, that campus security will be around. Yes, they are officers, but they're based on the campus and should be trained in interacting with students from all over, with all backgrounds. Unlike our trip for Mrs. Walters, again as Carrie mentioned, I've been to the campus to speak before and can explain why I'm... we're there. I can call security, any of us could, once we find this young man and his car."

"Okay," Mig said, begrudgingly. "That's the plan then. Except for figuring out what to tell the security people to get them to take him away so Clara doesn't go missing."

"Do you need me to go?" Carrie asked.

Peter glanced at her. "We could really use your help, Carrie. I think all of us are needed for this correction to go smoothly."

Mig said, "You don't want to go? I'm sorry, but I'm really excited about doing this. Not to mention, we get to help someone in a really amazing way."

Carrie's was nervous and afraid and knew it was showing. Mig added, walking to where Carrie was seated and putting his arm over her shoulders. She leaned against him, tipping a little of his coffee onto his shirt. He brushed it away and kissed her on the top of the head. "It'll be okay. I promise." He dabbed at a wet spot on her shirt.

Peter was pacing again, his voice deep and serious, "Carrie, it will be easier, likely safer, if you go. This Clara might be more comfortable talking to a woman than to one of us men, even if she does recognize me from my visit to Margaret's class. Plus, I may need Mig to back me up against Clara's boyfriend — or, whoever he is."

Carrie's worry grew at the thought of Mig and Peter cornering the potentially-dangerous young man. She knew Mig had a lot of street smarts — maybe more than Peter despite Peter's long life. She knew, too, and admitted it to herself, that Mig was a master negotiator, and keeping a situation from blowing up might depend on his skills to diffuse it. The whiff of an idea that Mig might be in danger, even a little, grew her worry again. She saw Peter looking at her, feeling as if he was looking through her again, and tried to empty her thoughts.

Mig grabbed her hand and squeezed. "Don't worry. Peter does all the work anyway, so you can't break anything, right, Peter?"

"I will. You two concentrate, or don't, and I'll get all three of us where and when we need to be. And back."

"It'll be okay," Mig said, and Carrie tried to relax. "You come along, and I'll have your back and you have mine. We'll both have Peter's because, you know, he's an old guy," Mig shot a look at Peter, ensuring Peter knew he was kidding. Peter chuckled.

Carrie bit at her lower lip. "I can't mess it up?"

Mig grabbed Carrie's hand, "Together, yes. To help people. Peter knows what he's doing. I'll be safe, okay?"

She squeezed his hand and sighed, then answered, "Okay."

"So, we're all going," Peter said, finalizing their discussion. "Finally, you'll both get the experience I want you to have."

With a rough plan set, and Carrie on board, they decided to make the trip sooner rather than later. "Be here tomorrow evening at 10 P.M. Instead of your Saturday lesson, you'll both get first-hand experience. In the meantime, I'll come up with what to tell the campus security when we call. I'll see you tomorrow night."

Arriving home, Peter went inside, closed the door, and locked it. He frowned, going over his thoughts and their conversation. He knew Carrie was right: they could intercept the student, maybe keep her safe for a day, but not necessarily long-term.

He decided that he needed to know what had happened to Clara Day. Walking purposefully to his office, Peter made a snap decision to go forward a few months, hoping Clara had been found by that future point so he could know what had happened to her.

He wouldn't even need to leave the house, he knew. He'd make a jump forward, use his computer in his office to find the truth, then come back, wake up in the morning, and be ready to travel with the Weathers.

14 – Preparations

The next morning, Saturday, proved hectic for the Weathers. Mig used the time to catch-up with customers via email. Carrie had several articles to finish. They parted ways at lunchtime — Mig driving to see a customer open on Saturdays, and Carrie hammering away on her keyboard.

Both were feeling accomplished when they called it a day. Mig returned home and they prepared for the late-night time travel adventure to come.

Peter was waiting at his front door when Mig and Carrie arrived at 10 P.M. Although he'd awaken in his bed that morning, Peter had stayed in the future for hours searching the news, and his sleep had been short-to-nonexistent. Despite this, his anticipating of traveling with both Mig and Carrie had him feeling reinvigorated.

It had been worth the lost sleep, though, as he now knew what to tell campus security. He'd found out what happened to Clara Day.

Mig and Carrie were keyed up for the trip, too. Mig more than Carrie, but even she said that she was less anxious than she'd expected, and she had carefully memorized the role she would be playing for Clara Day. With their upbeat mood, Peter decided they didn't need to know what Clara's boyfriend had done to her. He could tell them after they returned from the trip.

Carrie asked if Peter could explain again how they would approach the young man. She was worried, in case the boy was as dangerous as they were assuming.

Peter assured her several times that campus security was an integral part of their plan, and would ensure he and Mig's safety. Carrie's face showed relief every time he repeated it.

This part of the plan — to involve campus security — wasn't sitting well with Mig. He said, "I'm not sure about this, to be honest. If we call security on this kid, they'll probably arrest him, but they might arrest us."

Peter patted Mig's shoulder, and said lightly, "Well, let's be safe, not sorry. They're more likely to make us leave than do any arresting. Besides, I think your wife feels better knowing we won't be alone in confronting this young man."

"Yes, I do," Carrie said, smiling at Mig. "Let me make a quick run to the rest room and I'm ready to get on with this."

Watching Carrie leave the room, Mig asked, "What if he's innocent, Peter? What if Clara turns up, and she's been off staying with a friend or something. I hate to get this kid arrested, or us, if he didn't do anything."

Peter looked directly at Mig. "I'm going to tell you something I'd planned to tell you after, and I would prefer Carrie not know before we go."

Mig angled his head closer to hear Peter, with his peripheral vision aimed toward the door to ensure he could see when Carrie returned. "What is it?" Mig whispered.

"The young man took her, Mig. No doubt."

"How do you know? Have you..." Realization dawned in Mig's eyes. "*When* did you go?"

Peter whispered, "Yesterday when I got home, I went forward to find out what had happened to Clara. I wanted to understand what and who we'll be dealing with. Plus, I needed to find something about the man to use against him when we talk to campus security." He paused.

"And?" Mig pointed toward the doorway, reminding Peter they had little time before Carrie would return.

"Clara will be found, being held captive in his house, a few weeks from now. They'll arrest the young man — his name is Derrick Thornton — after he's caught while trying to rob a bank. Police will search his house and find Clara. They'll also find guns, evidence from another bank robbery, and such. The evidence against him was strong... will be strong. Clara will be safe with him sent to prison."

Mig's eyes darkened, "That's messed up."

"Yes, it is. Now, honestly, we could skip this trip because Clara will be saved without us. But, I need you two to get experience. Not to mention, we'll be saving Clara from the trauma. I'm confident he'll have a gun with him when he abducts Clara, our plan is to tell campus security he has a gun with him."

Mig nodded. "Okay. I get it. We'll follow your plan and call the campus security, tell them about the weapon."

Peter looked toward the door and whispered, "Don't tell Carrie until we return. She has to delay Clara, and she will have an easier time remaining composed if she doesn't know Clara's fate. Or, what her fate will be if we fail."

At that moment, Carrie returned. They were still huddled together, and she gave them a quizzical look. Mig smiled and distracted her by asking if she was ready to travel.

With a sigh, she said, "As ready as I'll ever be."

"Let's go then," Peter said, opening the panel and leading them into the time travel room.

Closing the panel, Peter repeated their plan, then asked, "Do you want to make any last-minute adjustments?"

Mig and Carrie both shook their heads.

"Okay," Peter confirmed, as he scanned his notes one more time, then placed them on top of a file cabinet.

Peter repeated the lesson on concentrating. He finished by saying, "Don't worry about being able to actually travel now.

You're traveling with me, so I will be the one focusing and pull you both along with me."

Peter sat down in the chair and asked Mig to stand on his left, Carrie on his right. He took a few deep breaths.

15 – Triad of Time

Carrie blinked. She, Mig, and Peter were standing next to a brick building. While it had been night when they entered the time travel room, Carrie saw it was bright day. Dizzy, she reached out toward the building to steady herself — momentarily thinking her hand might go right through it. It didn't, and she leaned against the wall taking deep breaths. The air stank of fried food and car exhaust; she wrinkled her nose.

After the dizziness passed, Carrie glanced around, happy to see no other people nearby. She saw that Mig and Peter were doing the same, shifty, glancing-around thing. *Not suspicious at all*, she thought sarcastically.

There were no windows on their side of the building, and trees blocked them from view on the other side. Still, the three stayed against the building and talked, trying to act like they were just having a routine conversation, to overcome any potential observers' confusion at their sudden appearance.

"Good spot, Peter," Mig said after confirming they had appeared away from prying eyes.

"Luck," was all Peter said.

Carrie walked to the side of the building and peered around. She could see pathways and several other buildings. Few students were moving about the campus. *Good timing, too*, Carrie thought.

"You two feel all right?" Peter asked.

Mig and Carrie exchanged glances, then both nodded.

"I feel normal," Carrie said. "Is that normal?"

Peter and Mig laughed. "Yes," Peter said. "Feeling normal is normal on a trip."

"It is," Mig said. "Except for knowing we don't belong here, and feeling connected back to our time. You can feel that, too. Right, Carrie?"

Carrie thought for a moment, her eyes glazing as she examined her internal feelings. "No," she said slowly. "I don't feel anything like that. Just... normal."

Peter stepped to the corner of the building, stopping next to Carrie, with Mig following until he could see around the corner.

Peter pointed, "I see the parking lot Margaret told me about, and that building there--" he shifted his arm slightly to point at a large gray building, "is where Margaret is holding her class." He checked the time on his cell phone. "We have exactly fifteen minutes before her students are let out. We need to find this Derrick person, and Carrie needs to intercept Clara. Let's roll."

The three made their way along a sidewalk toward the gray building Peter had indicated. Carrie had to concentrate to keep herself from tiptoeing and glancing around. She knew they didn't need to be stealthy at this point, but her heart was beating fast and she was compelled to adopt a "sneaky" posture.

Mig patted her back, and she realized she was sneaking again. Straightening and walking more slowly, she fell into step behind the two men where she felt less obvious.

Mig and Peter approached the parking lot, then stopped several cars away from an old Mustang idling in a handicapped space. Carrie caught up to them and followed their gaze. An unkempt young man sat behind the wheel. "I think that's him," Mig said, nodding in the car's direction. Peter looked the vehicle over carefully, then agreed. The two walked slowly along the parking lot until they were past the car, Carrie following, her eyes on the sidewalk to avoid staring at their target.

The men stopped at the building's door and turned around to face Carrie. "That's got to be him, Mig. Did you see his posture?"

Mig nodded. The car's driver had been leaning forward, his face almost to the windshield, staring at the gray building. It was the posture of someone lying in wait.

"I'm gonna go to the classroom now, so I can intercept Clara," Carrie said.

Mig pulled his cell phone from his pocket and dialed. "I'm calling campus security. Right behind you, Peter."

"Okay," said Peter, retracing his steps toward the parking lot. "Mig and I will go have a talk with that young man. Stall Clara as long as you can, Carrie."

Peter and Mig approached the parked car as Carrie slipped into the building. When they reached the car, they could hear it idling, and the man's gaze was still fixed on the gray building. Peter stood in front of the car to block Derrick's view of the building's doors.

Mig walked around the back of the car, finished his call to security — who had confirmed they were on their way — and stealthily blocked the driver's side door.

Just as the young man sat back and honked his horn at Peter, Mig tapped on the driver's window.

"Go away," the young man said. He waved angrily at Peter, who didn't move. Instead, Peter crossed his arms and stared at the driver.

Mig rapped on the window, harder this time. "Open your window now. Campus security," Mig lied.

"Go away," the driver said again, but he rolled his window down an inch. "What do you want? I'm here to pick up my girlfriend. I'm not doing anything. Leave me alone."

Mig heard the defensive tone in his voice, but he also heard it waver a little. In an authoritative voice, he said to the driver, "If you didn't want to be bothered, you shouldn't have parked in a disabled parking space," Mig growled. "You're not going anywhere with anybody until you talk to us."

The young man looked surprised, then said, "I didn't see the sign. Anyway, I'll be leaving in a minute. I just need a minute."

Mig got the impression this wasn't the first time the driver had been approached by authorities — real ones, not imposters like he and Peter. Mig tapped on the window again, "Please step out of the car."

With another sigh, the driver complied and stepped out of the car. In an act of defiance, he slammed the door behind him. "What?" he yelled sharply at Mig, fixing him with a hard stare.

Mig stared back and took a step toward him. Then, he saw the driver blink. *Not so tough against men, are you?*

The real campus security arrived just then. Mig and Peter waived them over.

Carrie found Margaret's classroom quickly and stationed herself across from its door. For their plan to work, Carrie needed to delay Clara as long as possible.

When Clara came out with the other students, Carrie called her name and pulled her aside. Carrie lied that she was writing an article about Professor Margaret Bonner, and asked for Clara's impressions as one of Margaret's students. Clara was eager to share her positive opinion of the professor — "My favorite one!" — and talk about the class.

Carrie walked alongside Clara, who said she was heading to her next class, which would start in fifteen minutes. Carrie bypassed the parking lot by leading Clara to a campus-adjacent coffee shop, "where we can talk."

She kept asking questions and writing notes for the fictitious article until, pointing at her watch and apologizing,

Clara said that she needed to get to her next class. Carrie walked with her, guiding her the long way around the parking lot and into a flat, red-brick building where they said their good-byes.

Carrie jogged back to the parking lot to see how Mig and Peter were doing. As she approached, she saw campus security was already there. Two officers were speaking with Peter, and Mig was gesturing toward the young man. The young man was yelling, though she couldn't make out the words. She didn't even try. Her eyes were on Mig.

The campus security officers listened to Mig and Peter's pre-planned lie that they had seen the young man with a gun. As Peter had told Mig, from his going into the future, he'd known the presence of a gun in the car was likely.

A city police car pulled up. Its occupants spoke with a security officer briefly, then one began searching inside the car. He leaned back, held up a gun, and the other officer spun Derrick around and handcuffed him.

Mig and Peter breathed a collective sigh of relief as the young man was led away. One of the security guards thanked Mig and Peter for contacting them. Mig looked surprised as the guard shook his hand.

Carrie overheard one of the guards telling the now-captured man that he and his gun were going to be turned over to the city police.

After security drove away, Carrie approached and leaned in to hug Mig. "I'm so glad it's over," she said.

"I think we did good," said Mig, looking at Peter.

"I agree. It went smoothly for us, and as Clara isn't here, I'm assuming it went well for you, Carrie."

"Very well," she said. "I could even make an article out of my notes, if we want."

Peter rubbed his hands together. "Now, back we go."

Returning to the empty corner of the building where they'd arrived, Peter urged Mig and Carrie to focus, just for practice, and he would get them all home.

Carrie closed her eyes, and a moment later felt a puff of air, smelled the freshly-washed baby fragrance, and heard a muffled sound like a light bulb blowing out, followed by silence as they returned to their own time.

16 – Sunday

Mig awoke first and rubbed Carrie's shoulder. She stirred awake and turned toward him. "Good morning," she said, planting a kiss on his lips.

"Wow, time travel stuff is intense," Mig said.

"Amazing," Carrie agreed, shaking her head.

They decided to get up and have breakfast, even though it was early, just after 5 A.M.; but, they were wide awake. Mig wanted eggs and fried potatoes, and suggested they head to the diner downtown. Carrie knew that they were out of potatoes, and agreed.

They showered, dressed, and headed out without checking to see if there was news about Clara. They knew there shouldn't be.

As they ordered their food, they felt a little disoriented. Mig tried to order a Monday special before the server reminded him it was Sunday. Clara's disappearance from the college had been on a Wednesday. They had taken their trip back-in-time on Saturday, and now they were back and it was Sunday, four days after Clara's disappearance, which they'd undone.

Their ordering almost took longer than the food, which was placed in front of them within minutes. They ate and talked about everything but their trip.

Carrie was astonished things could feel so normal after they'd hopped back and forth through time less than 24 hours ago. Aside from Mig's day-confusion, it was a regular breakfast out. She looked at Mig, and he stopped eating and returned the look. Whatever he saw on her face, he seemed to understand what Carrie was thinking. "I know," he said, "seems like we should feel weird. I don't. Do you?"

Carrie shook her head. "Nope. It's just another Sunday."

After breakfast, Mig called Peter from outside the restaurant to see how he was, how Clara and his friend Margaret were, and Peter replied that everything was corrected just fine. Mig ended the call.

All the way home Mig posed time travel situations and Carrie responded. He went from serious situations to silly ones, and they were both laughing by the time they arrived home.

Their conversations about time travel were put on hold when their oldest showed up at their door with her family, bags of take-out food in hand.

Lunch with Mig's daughter Nicole, her husband, and the grandchildren went from being just lunch to being a movie marathon. Mig found himself biting his tongue several times as he almost said something time travel related to Carrie. Knowing what they knew, and wanting to talk about it to each other, they also knew they mustn't discuss it within earshot of their family. With the long visit, Mig began to wonder how they would keep their time travel work hidden from their kids.

At one point, Nicole asked Mig why he and Carrie were so jumpy. He brushed it off as "looming news deadline," but knew he and Carrie would need to, in the near future, find a way not to look like they were busting at the seams around the kids.

Their family headed home just after 10 P.M. What questions Mig could remember biting back in front of the kids, poured out after they'd gone, and he and Carrie stayed up into the wee hours talking.

Peter awoke feeling hopeful Sunday morning. Now that both of his time travel students had experience under their belts, the next step was to bring them up-to-speed on the serial killer and enlist their help.

The photo Roman had given him drove him to distraction, and he soon set aside his research on the serial killer. He gravitated toward research on his own family, and sought to find more information on Roman.

Peter ended up searching his grandfather's papers. He didn't find much about family, save one photograph of his grandfather and mother standing with a man Peter had never met. A note on the back read, *1950-Alfonso, Renee & Manuel* — the latter would be Peter's great-grandfather, and the same man shown in the photograph from Roman.

Peter would have been about twelve at the time of the photo. He didn't recognize the setting. Just as Peter and his Grampa had looked close to the same age, the two men in the photograph looked far too close in age to be different generations. Peter's mother, however, looked older than both of them. He knew she had stopped traveling years before the photograph had been taken, when she'd become pregnant with his brother, Simon.

Peter thought and paced. He wondered why Grampa hadn't told him more about his great-grandfather, who was obviously a time traveler. All Peter knew was that his great-grandfather had been named Manuel, and he had lived in New Mexico before moving the family to Colorado. Grampa had never mentioned their time traveling had come from him, nor talked about their ancestors. *In fact, Grampa gave me the impression he was the first time traveler, Mom the second*, Peter thought.

And what about Roman? He knew about time travel. Peter wondered how many other family members might be out there.

Putting away his Grampa's papers carefully, he forced himself to shift back to the looming problem. Silvia Andrews — so young, still lost — he had taken on as his responsibility, and he must find a way to correct her death.

He had taken too much time away from the chase, he knew. He didn't need to train Mig and Carrie until they were experts. They didn't even technically need to know the details of time travel. He wasn't entirely sure himself why he was teaching them so much. Maybe because it was nice to be able to talk with them, after his Grampa's years-long absence. Or, maybe it was because Mig had been so quickly able to *do* what he could.

Unfortunately, he'd taken so many weeks that there was now a looming deadline that would lengthen the delay. Peter was committed to take a trip, a plain old plane trip across the country without time travel. He had agreed to present at a New Mexico paranormal conference scheduled for the first week of November, and would be away for several days.

Checking his calendar, Peter saw October was almost gone. He was ticketed to fly out on Monday — which was less than a week away! He emailed Mig and Carrie to give them a heads-up that he'd be away.

He needed to get on with it. The more women this serial killer destroyed, the more ripples when it was all corrected. He had to tell Mig and Carrie about the serial killings, and that he wanted their help to correct them all. It was time.

Saturday, he thought. *I'll tell them this Saturday.*

17 – Three Murders and A Lesson

Listening to the news early on the first Saturday of November, Peter heard the anchor announce that another woman's body had been found, and police suspected foul play. Again, an old watch was found with the body. "The Sheriff's Office issued a statement that they believe the same killer is responsible for other recent murders in Nash County."

Peter turned off the television just as Mig and Carrie pulled into his driveway. *Today's the day*, Peter thought. *I'll let them know I have a serial killer to stop, and I've recruited them to help.* He sighed, *And another woman to save.*

Once Mig and Carrie had coffee in-hand, Peter started by showing the Weathers a news article on the new murder. Details were slim, the article reporting the early morning discovery of a woman's body near Middlesex. Police were investigating, it read, and the body had been identified as that of Tamsin Hawthorne, 24, who had recently moved to North Carolina from the UK.

"Her family has been informed," Carrie read. "That must be awful, not just to lose their daughter, but to be an ocean away. So sad."

The last paragraph described an antique watch found at the scene. "That detail," Peter said, "about the watch matches two other murders under investigation already. Instead of a lesson, I'd like to have you two help me with research, so we can plan to travel back and stop this serial killer before he kills any of these young women. It's a problem I've been having trouble solving, and three heads will be better than one."

"*Murders* to correct?" Carrie said, her voice quavering with distress.

"Not right now, Carrie. I'm just making you both aware of these women's murders, but this isn't something we'd correct tonight. These killings go back to September and we need to plan, not tackle them today."

Carrie took a few deep breaths, then nodded.

Peter continued, "The article confirms similarities of this third murder with two others, including mention of an antique timepiece left with the body. I've heard through a doctor friend, who knows the coroner, that the murders are being treating as serial killings. He's the one who gave me details on the watches. It isn't mentioned in the article, but I happen to know the watches were found in their mouths. All timepieces were over a hundred years old."

"Three women killed near here by the same person," Mig stated, and Peter confirmed.

Carrie clenched her hand, pressing it against her chest over her heart.

"Three young women, all found in Nash County, and all since September. I've been following it since the first woman, Silvia Andrews was found the first of September, followed soon after by another young woman, Valerie Edmonds. It was the watches that caught my attention."

Carrie paled. "That's just creepy."

"A serial killer and antique watches? It's not you, is it, Peter?" Mig's tone made it clear he was joking.

Carrie shivered anyway.

Peter set the article aside with a sigh. "No, but thank you for that, Mig," he said sarcastically. "I'd like to make this serial killer's actions be our focus for today. Soon we'll need a plan to stop him, as I've tried and failed to do so. It will take all of us, I think, to create a plan that can work. Are you ready to begin?"

Mig nodded, then nudged Carrie. "Mig, this is a big, scary deal, but I'll help. How do we get started, Peter?"

Peter explained the research he needed, and Carrie scribbled notes as he talked. After about five minutes, Carrie said, "Okay, I'll see what I can find out."

Mostly, she was glad Peter only wanted research right now. She wasn't ready for a time jump that might involve the three of them facing down a murderer.

With Mig and Carrie up-to-speed on the murders, after they left Peter drummed his fingers on his desk, thinking. *Even if he does kill again, we will plan to stop him before he kills Silvia Andrews. Time is on our side.*

After reviewing what he'd taught the Weathers so far, and their performance on the trip for Clara Day, he decided they knew enough to proceed. He could do the traveling and bring them along. If Mig was able to control his travel, that was a bonus, but not required.

Once the three of them reviewed Carrie's research, and his notes, they would set a plan and go.

18 – Research Time

Sunday morning, Carrie awoke and found herself alone in bed. She yelled, "Looks like I'll be busy today researching for Peter."

From the bathroom, Mig responded, his voice muffled by his toothbrush, "You don't need me, right? I think I'll mow the grass today while you're busy."

"Mowing sounds like a lot more fun," she said, and climbed out of bed. Groggily, she joined him in the bathroom, pausing to kiss him on his cheek, avoiding his toothpaste-ringed mouth.

While Mig made coffee, Carrie sat down on the couch with her laptop computer. She started by reading news articles about the murders published online. She reviewed photographs included with the articles, noting which police departments were shown at each site, and downloaded the available police reports.

By the time Mig had finished his coffee and headed outside — stooping to give her a kiss on the way out — she was printing each of the women's obituaries. She made a note to scan social media for photos and posts by the victims' families, or comments from their online friends. This task wouldn't provide much information to her quest, she knew, and would sadden her more than anything, but she wanted to be thorough.

***

Carrie ordered a pizza, and at 2 P.M. the delivery woman arrived and she set her work aside. Mig was just putting away his mower.

Mig came inside and hugged her one-handed, taking the pizza from her with his other hand. "Thanks for ordering food."

"No problem," she said. "I was tired, and figured you would be too from all your yard work."

"I'm okay," Mig said, dripping sweat on the kitchen floor as he set the pizza on the counter.

"Good. Then, let's eat and I can tell you how my research went."

"Sounds good to me. But, right now I need a shower. Mowing was sweaty work."

After showering, Mig found Carrie clicking away on her laptop, stopping intermittently to take a bite of pizza. He grabbed a slice and sat down on the couch, looking at her laptop screen. "What's that?"

She leaned back against the couch. "I'm checking... um, remember that Peter said Roman asked for help because his children had died? I tried looking them up, based on the notes Peter gave me. But what Roman told Peter makes no sense. Here, look at this."

She turned the computer so Mig could see her screen. "Here, where Roman said his two children were killed. You see it? This report says there were several children injured that day but only one death. And the child that died was the son of a local teacher, not Roman. Plus, I haven't yet found any records of Roman that show him with a wife or children, not even in census records where he shows up. I think he lied to Peter about all of it."

Mig read the article on the screen, then looked at Carrie. "So, why did he come to see Peter?"

"I think that's the big question." Carrie said. "And I don't think the answer will be one that's good for Peter."

"Or us," Mig said, picking up his cell phone and dialing.

Ending the call after a few minutes of discussion, Mig said, "Peter's on alert now. He said to thank you for checking on Roman's story. He can't figure out what Roman's up to, any more than we can. Oh, and he said you're awesome."

Carrie smiled. "I heard him, Mig. I'm sitting *right here*."

He leaned in for a kiss, locking eyes with her. As he turned away, she mused, "I wonder what Roman is up to."

"Not something good," Mig said, picking up his slice of pizza. "But we've got Peter's back."

19 – Chile Today

Peter spent his Sunday online searching for a cabin to rent in New Mexico; something he'd forgotten to do when he booked his flight. He was making the most of his time away by renting a small off-grid cabin, and staying for a few days before and after the conference.

Although he was growing impatient with himself over the lag in dealing with the serial killer situation, he knew he could use his time away to review Carrie's research and fill in gaps in their plan. The details weren't yet set, but they knew they would go back to the first of September before Silvia Andrews was killed, save her, and try to identify the killer. There would be work to follow, ensuring the authorities captured the man before he went after Valerie.

Looking over his bank account and assets brought his Grampa to mind, as he had been the one who'd taught Peter to keep track of money and check balances after traveling. Grampa had used his own time-travel knowledge to make good investments and Peter lived frugally to keep them growing. As long as he was careful, his savings would be enough to take care of him for his very long lifetime.

He wondered how his grandfather was faring off in the future. He knew the old man could take care of himself, yet worried anyway. Not for the first time, Peter considered taking a trip forward to visit his grandfather, then dismissed the idea. His Grampa went off to retire. It was one thing to ask him questions via the classified ads, and quite another for Peter to show up at his door in the future, even if it was about family. With Roman likely up to something, Peter wished he could air his concerns to the only trustworthy family member he had left. *Then again, didn't I recruit the Weathers so I could have help without wearing out Grampa?* But, no, he knew connecting with them was about time travel. Peter's Roman problem was about family.

But then, Grampa wasn't the only one he could ask, he suddenly remembered. In the note he'd left for Peter, Grampa had mentioned someone named Adell. Maybe his best bet was to go where Grampa had told him to go! He slapped his forehead.

If he found this Adell, he might get his questions answered. As soon as he returned to North Carolina after the New Mexico conference, he would follow his grandfather's instructions and go to past-New Mexico — and invite Mig and Carrie to come along.

The day before Peter was to fly out to his conference, Mig suggested they invite Peter over for lunch. "I think it'd be cool if we could hear more of his stories today. The more we learn the *how* and *what*, the more I want to hear the *why* and *who*. And I want to make chile!"

"Sounds good to me," Carrie said. "I want to hear about traveling for reasons *not* related to murder victims! You can make your famous green chile while I grill up burgers and we'll have Mexican Hamburgers. Let Peter taste your hot chile, finally."

Mig placed the call, and as soon as he'd suggested story time and chile to Peter, he'd agreed, responding, "I'd love to!" loudly enough that Carrie heard him through Mig's phone from halfway across the room.

Soon after, Mig hung up the phone. He was laughing. "Peter knows Mexican hamburgers. He said he hasn't had any kind of smothered burritos since his Grampa left, and that he can't wait to try my pork green chile."

Before Carrie knew it, it was noon and Peter was knocking on their front door. She opened it and asked, "You hungry?"

"Pretty hungry," Peter said. "Tell me about your husband's famous pork green chile."

Laughing, she shook her head and pointed Peter toward the kitchen. "He's just cutting up the pork now. Why don't you join him? We can talk while you watch him prepare his famous concoction." She put *famous* in air quotes.

Mig welcomed Peter. "Glad you could make it."

"Oh, I wouldn't miss it. I'm intrigued." Peter's eyes scanned the counter, which at the moment contained plates of raw meat, spice jars, and a mysterious freezer bag.

Carrie said, "I'll be right back. Don't start telling stories without me." She grabbed a plate of hamburgers and went out the screen door to the grill.

"Keep it on low," Mig yelled after her. "I don't want those burgers burning up before the chile's done. Peter might not like them burnt the way we do."

In a few minutes, she returned smelling of smoke. "Burgers are on the grill. *On low*, Mig."

"Looking forward to having Mexican Hamburgers. It's been a while," Peter said.

Mig held up the plastic baggie, full of something green and squishy looking. "We grew these chiles last year, roasted them, peeled off the skin, and froze them. I pulled them out of the freezer about an hour ago, and we'll be adding them to the pork in a little while after I brown it."

Peter took the bag, examining the tender roasted peppers inside. "Nice. Are they hot?"

"That depends," Carrie said. "Yes, they are a hot pepper, except the peppers get hotter as the months go by. The Fall harvests are always the hottest, so it'll depend on whether those are summer picked or late picked."

"Interesting," Peter said.

Carrie handed him a fork. "Taste one. Let us know if you think it's hot enough."

Mig stopped Peter as he stuck the fork in the bag. "Wait a minute. Do it the right way." Mig grabbed a tortilla from a stack on the counter and tossed it on a paper plate. He warmed it briefly in the microwave, then tossed the plate on the counter. "Put a pepper in and roll it up."

Peter forked one of the roasted, skinned peppers and put it in the center of the tortilla. He rolled it up and took a bite. "Yeah, they're good and hot. Tasty." He smiled. "I haven't had roasted New Mexico chiles in years. I'd forgotten how good they are."

Carrie laughed. "Excellent. Wait until you taste Mig's chile."

Peter finished the last bite, then brushed his hands together. "Okay, Mig. Show me how *you* do this."

Mig prepared a pan and talked Peter through each step as he browned the meat, added the peppers, and stirred the simmering chile.

"Smells good, doesn't it, lad?" Mig said at the sound of Peter's stomach growling, either from hunger or the gut-bomb he'd ingested.

Carrie excused herself to check on the burgers, knowing story time wouldn't be starting while they were engrossed in cooking. She returned ten minutes later with the blackened burgers, and the men were still deep in discussion over the stove.

"That's pretty much it," Mig said as he stirred the thickening concoction, adding another sprinkle of flour as it bubbled.

Peter waved his hand over the chile, coaxing the steam toward him. "Man, that smells good." He breathed deeply, and Carrie suppressed a chuckle as he closed his eyes, taking in the smoky scent.

She set the table, complete with lettuce, tomatoes, cheese, sour cream, and a pitcher of tea.

"It's ready," Mig declared as he pulled a plate of warmed tortillas from the microwave. "Let's eat."

When the meal was finished, a sole burger languishing on a plate in the center of the table, Peter leaned back. "I can't eat another bite. But I want to. The chile was fantastic."

"Glad you liked it," Mig said, beaming. Carrie reached for his plate, and he handed it off before standing. They cleared the table in no time as Peter sat, sated and smiling.

"Okay, story time," Carrie announced.

"Right." Peter sat, one hand on the table and the other over his belly. He looked at the table, apparently surprised to see the clearing done, as Carrie refilled their glasses and sat opposite him. Mig joined them at the table, popping a bite of pork into his mouth as he took his seat.

"Well, I'll start with a simple correction. No murders involved, for Carrie's sake." Peter took a gulp of tea and cleared his throat. "I've been going through my files. I took very seriously your request for examples of how I've used time travel. There are three stories I've picked for today that I think will give you a sense of the possibilities. At least, it'll be a start. We'll see what you think, and I can share more examples at our Saturday lessons as we move forward.

"The first tale I have for today is of a one-and-done correction. It's similar to how I left a note to myself so past-me could stop Carrie from getting food poisoning. Well, not quite that simple, but still accomplished in one trip lasting just a couple of hours." He launched into his story, which involved his grandfather, a farmer, and two real estate transactions.

His grandfather had chanced across the farmer, his wife, and their baby when they were in fierce discussions with a police officer. The officer had apparently told the family to, "move along," when he found them sleeping in their car in an alley. Grampa intervened, bringing the family home with him, which is when Peter met the three — "I'm Bob Turner, this is my wife, Alma, and our baby boy is Bob Junior."

After much coaxing and a hot meal, Bob told his sad story to Peter and Alfonso. It had started, according to Bob — and confirmed by Alma — when Bob's parents died. Bob and Alma had their own farm in North Carolina before then, and things had been going well. The soil was good, and they'd harvested "bumper crops" without problems. When Bob's parents passed away, the parents' Texas ranch was discovered to be heavily mortgaged and the Turners had, to their misfortune, decided to sell their successful farm and move to Bob's parents' ranch to try and save it. "Besides," Bob had said, "They had livestock and we couldn't just leave them starvin'."

It had not gone well for them in Texas. After several years trying to keep up with payments, disease hit. Despite Bob's best efforts to have the cattle treated, most had died. What few he was allowed to send to market weren't enough to make loan payments. By December they'd been evicted, the family ranch taken by the bank, and Bob and his family — at Alma's insistence — had returned to North Carolina looking for a way to start again.

"That's when Grampa came across them. They were sleeping in their car, had no food for themselves, were out of clean clothes, and had no real destination."

Peter fixed a stare on Mig. "Now," he quizzed, "what do you think would be the best fix for this kind of situation?"

Mig responded immediately. "Tell the farmer to stay on his farm in North Carolina. Tell him to sell his parents' farm and cattle."

"Wait a minute," Carrie said. "This feels like a trick question. Did something go wrong at their North Carolina farm. Is that something you and your grandfather researched, Peter?"

"Good on both of you. Yes, Mig, that's a logical plan. And," Peter chuckled, "yes, Carrie, my Grampa sent me off to the county to check on Bob's farm. It turned out his farm was still producing, though it had been hit by a tornado the year after Bob left, which had left its new owners in trouble financially."

Peter paused for a drink of tea. Carrie and Mig were both leaning across the table toward him, waiting for the time-travel portion of the story to unfold.

"So, Grampa let the family stay in his house for a bit, and he stealthily interrogated them until he found what he called 'the missing piece of our plan.'" Peter used a deep, accented voice for this last part, which Carrie assumed must be him imitating his Grampa.

"What was the missing piece?" Mig asked.

"You'll never guess, so I won't quiz you. The missing piece was that Alma was extremely superstitious. She'd even consulted fortune tellers on a few occasions. One of which, I might add, she said had predicted she'd have a daughter, though that hadn't deterred her from her beliefs when a son arrived instead. Grampa decided since, from his observations Alma seemed to be able to sway Bob easily, our best bet was to pose as prognosticators and visit Bob and Alma Turner's farm in North Carolina just after Bob's parents had died," he nodded toward Mig, "and convince them to stay on their farm, and sell the Texas cattle ranch." He nodded toward Carrie, "Grampa also insisted that they purchase farm insurance for an impending disaster."

Peter laughed. "My Grampa really fell into the role. He even gave Bob the date of the tornado to come. Though to his credit, he warned them not to tell anyone else, 'lest they become feared as witches' afterward." Again, Carrie noted the deep, accented voice Peter used to imitate his grandfather.

"Wow," Mig interjected. "And?"

Peter rubbed his eyes, shaking his head and chuckling. "It worked, though. A simple solution to a complex problem that, years later, we verified had worked quite well by visiting Bob Junior's farm stand and chatting up the now-young-man. In fact, that was in the late 1950s when I was still fairly new to time traveling, and the last time I looked up the farm online, some of Bob's great-grandchildren had expanded the farm to include agritourism lodging alongside the still-going crops. Not a bad result."

"That's incredible," Carrie said, leaning back.

Mig nodded. "I like it. You make it sound easy-peasy."

Peter, still chuckling, held up his hand. "Oh, but it wasn't. So many moving parts. Family issues to deal with. Working Alma against Bob without causing them to argue. It took us a week of planning and chatty dinners with Alma and Bob to get the details for our correction. But I will never forget my Grampa in his fortune-teller persona. Fantastic performance."

When Peter finally ceased chuckling, Carrie leaned onto the table. "Tell us your next story. You said you had three for us, right?"

Mig leaned forward, too, and Peter launched into story number two of the day.

Following the farm-saving tale, came the story of a woman he'd saved from hard times by convincing her not to change jobs, and a final tale about saving a woman from being hit by a garbage truck.

In the latter, Peter's grandfather had sent Peter off on his own, after learning from a neighbor that their daughter was in the hospital. Pregnant, she had been hit by a garbage truck when it lost its brakes. Her injuries were numerous, and her pregnancy endangered. "Grampa and I went to see her in the hospital. Then, he sent me back to keep her from stepping into the street, as gracefully as I could since — as of that time — she didn't know me.

"It was a little tricky, trickier than Grampa knew at first, because at the time her accident had happened, I was in a shop nearby. I'd watched the ambulance arrive. I'd seen the aftermath.

"So, I had to decide whether to leave a note for myself-back-then to stop her, being as precise and descriptive as possible. Or, to travel back to stop her myself, then get away without anyone seeing two of me on the street. Unable to decide, I finally told Grampa of my dilemma.

"He laughed at me, actually laughed at me. 'My child,' he said, 'go and do the job. If anyone comes here and tells me they've seen two of you, I'll just say your identical cousin is visiting. Say the same if you're caught out.'"

When Carrie looked confused, Peter added, "*The Patty Duke Show* was popular on television at the time. You know, the identical cousins thing the show uses to explain how they look like twins but aren't? The trip I took was in nineteen sixty-something..."

"Oh, yeah," Carrie answered. I get it now."

Mig squeezed her hand, and to Peter he said, "You'll have to excuse Carrie. She's younger than we are and doesn't get our cultural references."

Carrie laughed. "I'm not *that* much younger. I get your references."

When Mig raised an eyebrow at her, she added, "Most of the time."

Peter finished the story. "After that, I traveled back, delayed her on the sidewalk by introducing myself and congratulating her and her husband — whose name I'd learned while at the hospital — and saved her from the accident.

"It turned out no one saw me with myself on the street, anyway, not even the past-me who was shopping across the street."

When they finally said their good-byes late in the afternoon, Carrie's mind was whirling with possibilities inspired by Peter's stories. As they waved at Peter's disappearing headlights, Carrie turned to Mig. "Now I know how the kids felt when they kept asking for extra bedtime stories. I want to hear more!"

Mig laughed, enveloping her in a hug, then rocking her side-to-side. "Yes, and you also know how the storyteller feels when they really, really want to stop. I think we wore the old man out."

20 – Lunch with a Liar

On his way to the airport on Tuesday, Peter met Roman at Manny's restaurant, again putting Roman off regarding time travel, assuring the older man that he was sorry about his children — which Peter knew from Carrie's research had not died and probably didn't exist — but could not help him. Peter didn't mention his trip, not wanting Roman to know his house would be empty.

Roman's behavior was passive, even though Peter was still declining to help. In fact, throughout the meal, the older man seemed almost jovial. *If his children were actually in danger, and he was really here for my help*, Peter thought, *he would be downright confrontational by now.*

Instead, the older man told Peter stories of their family. Peter kept his guard up as he listened, knowing he needed to take anything Roman said with a grain of salt.

Several times during the discussion, Peter felt the urge to face-palm or more frequently the urge to slap the older man. Roman commented on the servers' bodies in inappropriate ways. He ranted about everything from government to grocery shopping, finding fault somehow with them all. The final straw was when Roman tried to put his hand on the server's waist as she handed him the check. Peter reached across the table and grabbed Roman by the wrist as the server stepped backward. "I think we should go, Roman. I'll pay for our meal." Peter made a point of standing between Roman and the server as he passed her his bank card and the bill.

Peter steered Roman toward the door, standing at the register to block Roman from reaching the woman printing his receive. With the bill paid and his card returned, Peter apologized to the server, pushed Roman outside, and walked him brusquely to his car.

They departed amicably — another clue to Peter that Roman wasn't really there for Peter's help. Peter's best guess was Roman wanted to know more about him, and he didn't think it was meant in a good way.

21 – Plain Travel

Arriving in New Mexico, Peter picked up a rental car at the airport, and drove to the cabin he'd reserved. It was a good hour away from the city-based conference. The cabin he'd selected was secluded, the land around it perfect for walking and communing with nature. He wanted solitude to think — and no conference attendees near enough to knock on his door unexpectedly.

Checking in at the rental office in Cabin One, he noticed a German Shepherd lying on a large dog bed in the corner. "Is that your assistant?" he joked to the woman entering his information into the computer. Her name tag showed her name as *Mrs. Angela "Angie" Bly.*

Angie laughed. "Yes, if only Max knew how to change sheets, rather than just greeting everyone and begging for walks when I'm on lunch break."

Peter stood, shocked for a moment; then, before the woman could see it, he forced himself to smile, "Max, is it? I once had a dog I named Max. Must be a common name for German Shepherds."

The woman laughed. "I guess, although in *her* case it's short for *Maxine.*" She handed Peter his paperwork and a key. "Cabin Eight is all ready for you. Let me know if you need anything."

Peter thanked her. As he opened the exit door, he felt a nudge against his leg. He looked down and found Max, wagging her tail, tongue hanging out through her dog-smile.

Peter patted the dog with his free hand. Then, a thought came to him. He turned to Angie. "I don't suppose you'd let me walk Max for you at lunchtime, would you?"

Her face showing surprise, "Um, sure," she responded. "Actually, I'd appreciate that, and I think Max would, too. Looks like she's taken to you already."

As he walked to Cabin Eight, Peter thought about his dog. Yes, he'd had a dog named Max, once, but one of his timeline corrections had rippled unexpectedly and removed the dog from his life. In fact, *his* Max had given Peter the idea that a dog could retain a memory of a pre-correction event. He coincidentally had come across the dog later on, and Peter believed Max had recognized him, even nudged his left pocket looking for treats — which had been Peter's custom to carry when the dog had been his. That had led Peter to ponder corrections as they related to non-humans, though as yet he'd dedicated little time to it.

Peter began walking with the cabin owner's dog that day, and did each day except his conference day. Together they quickly learned the trail among the cabins.

Until Peter's final day in New Mexico, when the lunchtime walk ended with a crime scene. Poor Angie Bly had eaten her last meal.

That is, unless Peter corrected it.

Mig picked up his vibrating cell phone. "It's Peter calling," he said to Carrie before answering.

Peter said his conference presentation had gone well, and asked how they were doing. Carrie caught bits and pieces of the conversation.

Then, she saw Mig's face change. His eyebrows raised, then his brow furrowed as he frowned. Mig said, "uh huh" several times, nodding and listening intently.

Mig motioned for Carrie to mute the television and come and listen. She did, and stood at the kitchen counter, leaning over the phone. Mig turned his cell phone on speaker.

Peter's voice came through the speaker, "...Max along the river below the cabins. The dog led me to the body. Sadly, it was his owner, Angie Bly. She's been howling ever since."

Carrie looked questioningly at Mig. He held up his index finger in a wait-one-minute-and-I'll-tell-you gesture. "Hang on a minute," Mig said, then muted his phone. He looked at Carrie and said, "Peter found a body and reported it. The woman who owns the cabin he's renting was murdered. Police just left, and he called to fill us in."

Carrie stared wide-eyed at Mig, her mouth hanging open, trying to absorb what he'd just said.

He un-muted the phone and said to Peter, "Okay, I've caught Carrie up. Keep going."

"Well, I'm not sure what more there is right now," Peter said. I'm keeping Max in my cabin. The big question right now is, do I bring the dog back with me, or leave it here in case we can save his owner. He'll have a home again, in that case. Maybe he won't be howling so much."

Carrie's eyes widened. Peter's distraction with the dog, while he'd just found a dead woman, surprised her. Now was a time when they needed Peter to *focus*.

"What about the killer?" Mig asked, tossing a glance at Carrie.

Peter paused, then answered, "Not sure what the next step is. I'm not prepared to take a trip back to try to save Angie Bly yet. We all have work to do, and I'm coming back tonight." He paused. "I'll leave Max here for when we save his owner."

Mig started to say something and Peter cut him off. "Mig, there's more to this than I've said. When the coroner opened Angie's mouth at the scene, he pulled out a watch shoved down her throat. I saw it for a second, before police finished questioning me and sent me back to my cabin. The watch means her murder is connected to the women killed there in North Carolina."

"Are you sure?"

"I am. There is a strangeness to these murders there in Nash County. Now he's killing here during my trip? It can't be a coincidence. From my hometown there, to this far-flung cabin here, I feel like this killer is following me. He may even know what I do. Though, I'm not sure of that."

"What can we do?" Carrie yelled too loudly into the phone speaker."

"Gather what info you can find online about the murder out here, of Angela Bly. I'll call you later."

Peter didn't call later. Instead, as Mig and Carrie were getting ready for bed, they heard a knock on their door. Mig opened it to find Peter.

"Wow, welcome," Mig said, waving Peter in and closing the door behind him. Mig looked at Carrie, her worry was apparent in her eyes.

"How are you?" Carrie asked.

"I'm okay. Sadly, not the first body I've seen," Peter said, dropping onto the couch. "We're now up to three women here in North Carolina, within a few miles around us, and one by the cabin where I was staying. Before I jump to any more conclusions, I think we should compare notes about any other women murdered in a similar way."

"Okay," Mig said, looking at Carrie. His face held a grim expression that added to Carrie's already significant fear.

"There's work to be done." Peter looked at Carrie, then frowned and looked at the clock on his phone. "Oh, wow. Sorry. It's late. You're tired. I didn't think about what time it was. Let's pick this up tomorrow. Unless you two are busy?"

Carrie grabbed Mig's arm with one hand, wrapping her other hand around his.

Mig shook his head. "I'll cancel my appointments as quick as I can in the morning."

"Good. I'll be back then. Good night." With that, Peter stood and left, leaving Mig and Carrie in the living room, looking stunned.

"For an old man, he's a whirlwind. Wow. Well, big day tomorrow then. I'm off to bed. You coming?"

Mig locked the front door and followed her into the bedroom. "I wonder what he's getting us into *this time*."

Facing away from him, Carrie rolled her eyes at Mig's continuing wordplay with the word *time*.

22 – The Long Story

In the morning, a bleary-eyed Carrie walked out of the bedroom to find Mig and Peter already drinking coffee in the kitchen. "Do you guys ever sleep?"

"Good morning," Mig said, standing and giving Carrie a kiss. She smiled and returned the greeting.

"Good morning to you, too, Peter," she said as she poured coffee into her already-waiting mug.

Peter had just taken a drink, and raised his mug as a *hello*, his cheeks puffed with the large gulp of coffee he'd taken. He swallowed hard, then said, "Good to see you. Both of you. My days away felt like a long time."

"Yeah. So what about this new murder? What's going on?" Carrie asked.

"Eh, I need a little more time with my coffee before I'll be coherent, I think. But here's a start." He passed a stack of papers across the counter, fanning them out. "Here's my notes on the murder of Angie Bly. When you two are ready, I think we should head to my house and I'll give you what background I have on all the women whose deaths are connected. With Carrie's help, I think we need to search all fifty states. I need to be sure whether this man is going where I go, or I'm jumping to conclusions."

    ***

An hour later, freshly showered, Carrie sat with her research piled in front of her in Peter's office.

"Peter, how do you wanna do this?" Mig asked.

"Let's start dividing what we've got so far. We have room to spread out in here, and see what we can make of our serial killer hunt." Peter hung a county map on his office wall, sticking pins in what had been pristine woodwork.

Carrie cringed, then remembered something she'd read about Peter's house. "You know, I looked up your house's records and found an interesting bit of history. Did you know your grandfather bought this house in 1929? Those were crazy times, and Alfonso Horacio bought this house from a man who had committed suicide after the stock market crash. There was an article about his suicide in the local paper. Did you know that?"

"No," Peter said, his hand halting in mid-air. He shook his head, then continued pushing a pin into the county map. "He never said. But I would guess somehow time travel was involved. If he had the money to buy the house, and to perhaps purchase it soon after a suicide, there may have been some foreknowledge on his part."

"Hmm," Carrie responded. "Anyway, I thought that was interesting. Just passing it along."

"Treasure trove," Mig said under his breath to Peter.

Peter stepped back and surveyed the map on the wall. Pins covered it, showing locations related to the local murders. *Having news people on my side is a big help*, he thought. *We've filled in a lot of blanks on the victims.*

"Why can't you go back and make an anonymous call to the police?" Carrie asked. "Tell them where one of these women is going to be killed so the cops can go catch this guy."

Mig shook his head. "No, we need someone to get there while she's still alive. Police may not be quick enough."

Peter sighed, pinching the bridge of his nose. He then stepped toward the map. He pointed at a red pin, which marked where the first of the serial killer's victims had been found, Silvia Andrews. "This young lady," he began, his voice strained, "was not originally found here by Nashville." He moved his finger and pointed to an empty spot on the map. "She was found here, by a hog farm in Spring Hope. I took a trip back, and an unexpected dunk into a pond. I came back with less information than I'd hoped, but had apparently spooked the killer enough to move his victim."

Carrie sat down hard, her mouth agape.

Mig asked, "You took a trip?"

Peter nodded. "This was back in September before I contacted you two. I traveled to the early morning before her body was found. I tried to intercept him, but instead, he almost caught me. That was in Spring Hope. I arrived just after midnight and watched for him. I was close to where the body was going to be found. Silvia's body, and her captor, were there," Peter explained. "Whoever it was, they got the drop on me, which I wasn't expecting. I'm pretty good at being stealthy, and staying ahead of my quarry. But, not him! I got away, but it was a close call. I hid underwater in a pond and came back to my time but, unfortunately, I didn't get a good look at him."

Horrified, Carrie gripped Mig's arm. Mig patted her hand reassuringly, and motioned for Peter to continue.

"Then, I traveled back a second time, arriving earlier than on my first trip. Knowing his movements, the second trip I instead called the county sheriff's office from a public phone — which, let me tell you, took some doing to find. I had to go all the way to Rocky Mount to find one. Luckily, I arrived in the city at night so there were no people nearby to spot me, and I'd made sure in-advance there were no ATM cameras in the area."

Carrie shifted, gripping the edge of her seat, Mig's arm held tightly in her grasp.

Peter took a breath and sighed heavily. "I told 9-1-1 that someone was going to dump a woman's body in Spring Hope along this road." Peter again pointed to the unmarked spot on the map. "I explained they needed to watch for him, and catch this killer dumping his victim around 1 A.M."

"What happened?" Carrie asked, her heart racing.

"Police didn't follow-up your tip," Mig mumbled.

Peter shrugged, "Yes, that's my opinion, too. When I called, the operator... um, dispatcher... whatever, asked me questions I couldn't answer. I didn't want to say too much, or inadvertently send their investigation in a wrong direction. I knew quite a lot less than we know now — thanks to you two. So, I lied that I'd overheard a man talking in a bar, then I hung up. What else could I say?"

"You tried, right?" Mig said.

Peter nodded. "I then prepared to end my trip and come back. As I did, from down the block I saw a Rocky Mount Police cruiser approaching. They had traced my call and sent police to look for me instead! When they couldn't find me, I hoped that they would be watching for the man to bring the body," Peter swallowed hard, "I hoped they would use my tip to watch for him in Spring Hope. But, they didn't. Her body wasn't found until morning, and not by the police."

"Wait a minute," Mig said. "You only called in a tip on your second trip through time? And you went to before your first trip, so you hadn't run into the killer, um, yet? And police came for you in Rocky Mount, but the killer still moved her body to Nashville? How would he know you'd tipped police off about Spring Hope?"

Peter's eyes grew wide. Carrie could almost see a light bulb appearing over his head as he reacted to Mig's question. "You're right. I hadn't registered that before. I didn't go near his Spring Hope drop site, and as far as I know the police didn't either, so why would he change to Nashville?"

"Mig, are you saying if the killer moved her body anyway, he knew about Peter's tip? Does that mean it's a police officer?"

Peter frowned. He tapped the red pin marking Nashville, "So he still changes his plans because he's a police officer or listens to police calls... No, if either of those were true, he would have *also* known the police were ignoring the tip and coming for me at the pay phone. They were nowhere near where he was leaving the body by the hog farm. No reason to change his plans. Why did he move her to Nashville after my second attempt?"

Peter pinched the bridge of his nose, then began pacing. "After my first trip failed was when I started to think that I needed help. I thought perhaps I wasn't as sharp as I needed to be. I couldn't solve the puzzle. After the second trip failed, I knew I couldn't do it alone." He turned and faced them, arms outstretched. "I'll be perfectly honest with you. My failure on correcting this, twice, is what compelled me to reconnect with you two, haunted house story and all. And here we are. Mig's question is an important one, and it's one that I hadn't thought of before now. This is the kind of help I hoped for when I chose to involve you."

"I'm sorry, what?" Carrie asked. Her stomach dropped.

"I apologize," Peter said. "I didn't believe I could tell you right away about the murders. Or that I had such plans for you. Perhaps I should have, and for not being up-front enough, I'm sorry. Please consider that, if I'd come to you with this serial killer issue when we met for dinner, likely you'd have walked out and never listened to me. You might have even thought I was a murderer."

Carrie opened her mouth to protest, but Mig grabbed her hand and pulled her into the hallway.

"I can't believe he's been using us," she said.

Mig kissed the back of her hand. "It's upsetting, I get it. But he's also right. If he'd said he was a time traveler and needed our help to stop a multiple murderer, we'd have been out of there quick. He did mention he could use help, too, so it's partly on us for not asking more specifically what kind of help. Don't you think?"

Carrie leaned her head on his shoulder. "I guess so. Well, what the heck do we do now?"

Mig squeezed her tightly, swaying side to side. "I think..." He stopped speaking, silently rocking with her. After a minute, he sighed. "I think, sweetheart, we keep on rolling. We are where we are, even if Peter got us here in a less-than-forthright way. We were helping him a minute ago. I say we keep helping."

He pushed her away until he was looking down into her eyes. "Besides, I think we've gotten more out of his teachings than he's gotten from us so far, don't you think?"

Carrie sighed. She knew he was absolutely right. They'd become time travelers! All Peter had gotten so far was a job teaching them and some research. "I'm still upset," she said, but nodded. They returned to Peter's office, where they found him seated behind the desk, his face pale.

"Okay, Peter. Yeah, it would have been nice to know sooner, but things are what they are. Don't be going back to change when and what you told us. We're good."

Mig looked at Carrie. "Well, we are mostly good. Don't be surprised if Carrie hides a chunk of Carolina Reaper pepper in your chile some day. But let's keep going. What's next?"

Peter stood and bowed toward the two of them. "I appreciate your forgiveness." Relief replaced the paleness on his face.

"Just tell me what I can do right now to help stop this killer," Carrie said, her voice strained but friendly.

"The three of us are going to stop him," Mig said. "Right, Peter?"

Peter raised his arms above his head, and ran his fingers through his hair as he turned and stared angrily at the map. Carrie saw shades of his Spiky Hair Guy persona. She didn't think he was acting now, but genuinely flustered. *This killer would make anyone crazy,* she thought, *especially if you have the power to stop him but can't find a way.*

Mig stood up and approached the map, standing next to Peter. "What if we tried it another way?" Mig asked. He pointed at a blue pin they'd placed to show where one of the victims was taken. "What if we went, to where this victim... this young woman," Mig corrected himself, "was last seen? We get there and confront him before he can take her away. Assuming he'll be coming to grab her, and that we know what she looks like, can we try interrupting him then?"

Carrie stood abruptly. "Mig, I don't like the idea of confronting a serial killer at night in a parking lot," she said, her voice breaking. "Just because he's only killed women doesn't mean he wouldn't hurt you guys, too. Or worse."

Mig looked at Carrie. She saw the concern for her in his eyes. "I'm okay," she assured him. "Just wanting a safe plan."

Peter was still pondering the map and the blue pin Mig had pointed out. "Hmm," was all Peter said.

Carrie suggested. "I'll dig around, and see if there are any bits of information we can add. Give me some time to look into the emergency call Peter made, maybe double-check where each woman was last seen on social media. Okay?"

"Sounds like a good next step," Mig said.

They both watched Peter. Instead of responding, Peter, apparently thinking out loud, began running through a series of options. "We call the police and report her as committing some minor crime, they arrest her. Another woman might be taken.

"We call and report a strange man, who we have no description of, and the police arrest the wrong person. Then, the woman could still be taken, or another woman taken from somewhere else.

"We go and observe, but don't call the police. Instead, we try to identify the killer without interfering. The woman likely still gets taken and killed, but we might discover who the killer is, what car he drives, and..."

Peter trailed off and looked at Mig.

Both men returned to the map. Carrie put her head in her hands, secretly wishing they weren't there with this time traveler trying to stop a murderer. A multiple murderer, no less, and Mig was talking with him about the best way to go into danger.

"We're gonna die trying to catch a serial killer," she whispered, covering her face with her hands. Realizing she'd said it aloud, she lifted her head. Mig and Peter were both looking at her.

"We can be safe, and stealthy, Carrie," Peter said.

Carrie stared at him, her eyes fearful. "What if you both die? Or Mig dies and you come back alone? You save this woman, this stranger, but make me a widow?"

As soon as it was out of her mouth, Carrie realized how cold it sounded. "I didn't mean it that way," she whispered. "Of course, I don't want you or Mig to be in danger, Peter. I'm... I'm just afraid. This man you're chasing kills. You said he almost caught you once already. This is a lot to think about. I'm sorry if I... I'm going to take a break from this gruesome..." Carrie stood and went upstairs to Peter's kitchen without finishing her sentence.

Mig listened to Carrie's footsteps up the stairs, then said, "She's just overwhelmed, Peter. Plus, she's a worrier. You've probably noticed by now."

"I've heard worse," Peter said. "I'm surprised she lasted this long today with as anxious as this makes her. She's probably more upset because I didn't tell you why I wanted you to be time travelers, before now."

Mig shrugged. "It's kinda messed up. But, she and I know you've done a lot for us. I wouldn't change a thing."

Peter rubbed his eyes. "Thank you."

Mig stared up the stairs toward the kitchen. "She's got a good heart."

Peter harrumphed, "You don't need to convince me. I see it."

Mig cocked his head. "You know, one of these days, maybe after we deal with your serial killer problem, you can tell us the real reason you picked *us* to help you."

Peter looked away. "I will someday."

Mig sighed and clapped Peter on the shoulder. "What about Carrie's suggestion, then? What if we call it a night and give her time to do more research, even if it's only to give her a break? Sound okay to you?"

"When did she suggest that? I didn't hear... Yes! It sounds like a good idea. We'll take a break... It won't hurt to get my thoughts in order, too."

Mig clapped Peter on the back again. "Then let's go join her in the kitchen and let her know."

Carrie was pleased to hear the ball was being put in her court. She'd gather as much information as she could, so the three of them would set as safe a plan as possible. She promised she would get a grip on their new reality, and be ready to face whatever they must do.

The three then talked of things that weren't time-travel related, and Peter broke out a jug of iced tea. As they spoke, Carrie's stress level fell. By the time she and Mig left for home, her anger had dissipated. She apologized to Peter for her outburst, but he refused to accept it. "I'm the only one who needed to apologize."

Before backing out of the driveway, Mig extracted a promise from Peter that he would not take action on his own.

When the Weathers arrived home, Mig held Carrie as they drank coffee; Mig brewed up a pot despite it being almost dinnertime.

"I feel awful. I didn't mean your safety was important and Peter's wasn't. I was just..." Carrie trailed off.

Mig kissed her on the forehead. "I know. Peter knows. Don't worry about it.

"And don't worry about this correction, either. We won't be crazy about it, or plan something you don't agree with, okay?"

Carrie's eyes watered, and she started to cry. She leaned her head on Mig's shoulder. "I just can't stand the idea of losing you. What would I do without you?"

Mig hugged her hard, then pulled a blanket off the edge of the couch and covered her feet with it. He held her until she stopped sobbing, making sure she was covered and removing the mug from her hand so she didn't drop coffee in his lap.

23 – Bad Vibes

Peter devoted Sunday to the Roman problem. Despite the good weather, he stayed inside, thinking, and digging through his grandfather's papers again.

Many things bothered Peter, not the least of which was that Roman had said he'd come because of Mig's photograph of the time travel room's glow. *What string of events had to fall into place for Roman to see the photo?* Peter wondered. *Why would he be reading a small-town news site from so many states away?*

Peter's mind buzzed with dozens of questions, but he had no concrete answers. *Has he been stalking me?* This was the most important question, in Peter's mind.

As if Peter's thoughts had materialized him, Roman stopped by that afternoon. His arrival took Peter by surprise, again, and Peter quickly grabbed his keys. He suggested they go to lunch. Roman hesitated, finally agreeing as Peter all but barred his front door. Peter didn't want him inside, and was glad when Roman got the message.

Once they were seated in the local diner, orders placed, Roman launched into family stories again.

He told Peter of visiting with his grandfather Alfonso when they were both young children. The family gathered, he said, in New Mexico where the older generations were living at the time. Roman's grandfather was alive then. "His name was Fire, really. Not the best of names, but it suited him."

Peter noted the unusual name, hoping he might set Carrie on the trail of family records at some point.

Family groups tended to stick together — some stayed in New Mexico, another group moved to Colorado — yet it was only Peter's grandfather and his daughter, Peter's mother Renee, who had separated and gone to North Carolina.

Roman said to Peter firmly, "You have chosen not to have children, no? You are much younger than I, and you look far younger than your years. That will help in finding a suitable woman to give you children." He chuckled.

Peter repulsed. Something in the older man's chuckle, and the arrogant words preceding it, disgusted him. Peter had lived through the decades when treating women as objects was the norm, and he'd known better, knew it was wrong long before the world — at least the thinking people in it — had caught up to him.

Peter felt a chill run up his spine. The serial killer they were hunting was leaving watches with the bodies. Peter thought, *What if the old watches are a message that the killer is a time traveler? Is Roman the killer we're chasing?*

Peter's mouth went dry. He kept his expression neutral, and Roman continued talking unabated.

As they were leaving, Roman's cane caught in a sidewalk crack and he fell to the ground before Peter could catch him. The old man cursed repeatedly as he struggled to get up. Peter grabbed his arm and gently helped Roman to his feet.

"Thank you," Roman said, his breathing fast, his voice a whisper. He took several deep breaths, then continued to his car as if nothing had happened. "I'll see you again soon, cousin," he said as he dropped into the driver's seat and shut the door.

Peter stood, watching the car drive down the street and out of sight. Anger rose in his chest. The deep, cursing voice, even the words themselves, had struck a familiar chord. He'd heard them before, coming after him down a hill near a Nash County pond.

Was he sure? Could he say he was absolutely sure it was the same voice? Yes, this man was a liar. Why would he be killing women, though? True, Roman was old-fashioned, misogynistic, and in ways unlikable. But he appeared frail to Peter, and Roman was older and much more frail than Peter's "retired" grandfather. Was it all an act?

He shook his doubts about the voice away, but they came back. Peter wasn't ready to call his memory of the deep voice a confirmation of his suspicions. Not yet. But the evidence against Roman seemed to add up.

On Tuesday, the news informed Peter of another murder. He decided a trip to the latest crime scene was in order.

He called Mig. This couldn't wait until the weekend. It was Tuesday and he wanted to go before the killer, Roman, or whomever it was, had a chance to kill again.

24 – Crime Scene

When Mig and Peter arrived at their destination just after midnight on Tuesday morning — less than a day into the past — they found the killer's latest victim just where the news had reported it found. Four women murdered now within Nash County. Plus, Angie Bly in New Mexico, the serial killer was up to five now. It made Mig sick, feeling as if they had caused their deaths by failing to stop the murderer.

Mig shone his flashlight along the ground. The woman's red hair was matted with mud and leaves. Mig stood away from her body, the light shaking slightly in his hand, and he mouthed a prayer. Then, he watched, horrified, as Peter reached a gloved hand into her mouth and extracted a watch from her throat.

"He's probably long gone," said Peter, oblivious to the horror he was causing. "She feels like ice and the blood on the watch feels dry."

"Isn't that, um, tampering with evidence?" Mig asked. He stepped backward to further distance himself from the sight, glancing around to double-check no one was around to see them.

"Maybe," Peter said, "but I need a closer look at this watch. All the other ones, the police locked up along with the bodies. I have a doctor friend who tried, and failed, to get a look at them. Closest I got was the one I saw them find on Miss Bly." Peter gulped so hard Mig heard the click in his throat.

Peter carefully turned the watch over, flecks of dried blood landing on his gloves. Mig's flashlight beam flickered off the silver, as for a moment he caught a whiff of blood. He made a gagging sound.

"Don't do that. You'll make me throw up," Peter said.

The light disappeared for a moment as Mig stepped to one side, covering his nose and mouth. He asked, "What can the watch tell you? Is it unique?"

Peter turned the watch over in his hand. "Well, if by unique, do you mean having the inscription 'P.H.B.' Those are my initials." He held up the watch.

Mig leaned down to get a closer look. The watch read, *To Emma. P.H.B.* "Those are your initials? Who would engrave your initials? Aren't you just being paranoid?"

"I don't think so. The watch is old, but the engraving looks shiny and new. This is bad, Mig."

Mig looked down at the woman, pitifully sprawled amongst the leaves. "You don't know her, this Emma? Do you, Peter?" He shot Peter a puzzled look.

"Don't you recognize her, Mig?" He shook his head.

"She was one of the employees at Manny's restaurant when we had lunch. I think she was at the register when I paid. Twice, in fact, since we corrected Carrie's food poisoning from that lunch."

Mig shone a light on the woman's face. "This is..." but he didn't finish his thought.

Peter looked at the face, dead eyes staying skyward. "Three times, actually. I met Roman there for lunch, too."

Taking a plastic bag from his pants pocket, Peter pushed the watch into the baggie and closed the dead woman's mouth. He stood, carefully removing his gloves. he folded the gloves and dropped them into the bag before zipping it closed.

"If you take the watch, how will the police know it's the same killer?"

He looked at Mig and said, "I'm not worried about that right now. Especially since we're going to try to stop all these murders. What worries me is that the chance of a serial killer using a watch with his own initials seems slim, but his knowing *me* enough to use *my* initials? Or to kill someone we'd seen before? That's most likely in my mind." He sniffed at the air.

"I believe," he sighed and continued, "that even though time travel doesn't seem to play a part in this murder, I think the killer is familiar with time travel. And familiar with me. I think it may be Roman, even though he appears frail. Probably just a role he's playing."

"You sure?"

Peter nodded. "All that we've learned so far... Now an obviously antique watch has initials on it that happen to be mine? I am confident this is the work of someone who is not afraid to harm women, and may be coming after me," he swept his hand over the body on the ground, "right along with them."

Peter moved to Mig's side. "We should return home. We need a plan to correct all of this and save these women. Roman being able to time travel adds a level of difficulty that, while it explains my failures, means we need an airtight plan. One he can't undo. And before he can frame me."

Sitting in his kitchen Thursday evening, drinking coffee later than he knew was wise, Peter reviewed the plan so far. It was incomplete.

More than that, having a time traveler involved, there was one problem foremost in Peter's mind: the Weathers. Peter didn't want Mig and Carrie — their connection with him — to be lost. *Whatever happened, whoever goes back with me to save the women, to stop... Roman? The Weathers must be either traveling with Peter or in the time travel room.* This correction plan started with Silvia, and was going to ripple forward to save all the women who had died after he'd drawn Mig and Carrie into his time travel inner circle. Peter didn't want to lose them. Not again.

Roman had to be stopped on their first attempt together. The plan had to be perfect. He headed for the time travel room.

He hoped somewhere in their travels, there might be notes that could point him in the right direction.

He'd also compile a list of unknowns, in preparation for the necessary trip to find Adell. While his attention had been taken up by Angie Bly's and the latest Nash County murder, he wanted to be ready for when they traveled back to 1898 to speak to the mysterious Adell.

25 – Lost Memories

When the Weathers arrived at Peter's on Saturday morning. Tired from a mad rush with the newspaper, they were looking forward to a self-imposed holiday break later in the month, and turkey dinner with their family.

"Let's hope we can complete our travels and have this all done and behind us by then," Peter said as he poured three coffees.

Once they were seated at the kitchen counter, Peter launched into his findings on the new murder. "I think the woman killed this week, Emma, might have met her killer at the restaurant where she works. Worked."

"Another woman was killed this week? That's awful. When did it happen?" Carrie looked at him earnestly.

Peter stared at her. "I'm talking about Emma Morrison. She was killed on Tuesday. We went over her case Wednesday night and Mig traveled back with me Wednesday to see her body before she was found."

Carrie looked at him, puzzled, then she looked at Mig, who shook his head at her. "Peter, we weren't here Wednesday, and Carrie and I hadn't heard about an Emma Morrison being killed."

"Neither of you remember being here Wednesday?" Peter asked.

They shook their heads.

"The watch with Emma's name and my initials?" Peter raised one eyebrow.

"What?" they said together.

Peter felt the hairs stand up on the back of his neck. If neither of them remembered, and he did, then only one scenario made sense. *Roman wiped their memories to slow me down. They need to know, at least part of this, he decided.*

He said, "Another time traveler has changed the timeline. This man we're chasing is definitely a killer *and* a time traveler."

"This is news to me," Mig said.

"Chasing a killer? A time traveling killer?" Carrie's voice rose precariously high. Mig grabbed her hand, gave it a squeeze, and released it. She blew out a breath, and Peter hoped she would calm down.

"He must have changed something after Mig and I traveled back, so you don't remember. I was in my time travel room most of Thursday. Fell asleep in there while making notes in my files and my grandfather's, woke up in bed." He searched his memories, shocked to find some sessions with the Weather had become smoky, new nights alone in their place. Peter snapped his fingers. "I have notes from our travels in my office, and copies in the time travel room. Let's go take a look. I need you both to remember. Well, I need to fill you in all over again, because you were here Wednesday, and we took a trip that night to find out more about Emma Morrison's murder. I have new notes I made yesterday, and they'll be no good if you don't remember everything."

He led them down to his office. Peter saw immediately that the wall map was missing. No map. No pins marking where the women's bodies were found. The notes on his desk were gone, too, save two pages of notes on the first murder.

Peter stood behind his desk as Mig and Carrie sat down. "Carrie, when I arrived and told you about Emma Morrison, you said 'another woman,' so you must remember at least one woman's murder. Tell me what you remember. Do either of you remember talking with me about a serial killer?"

"Sure," Carrie said. "I saw it on the news months ago. I think her name was Silvia, right?"

Peter nodded, and Mig continued, "I don't remember us talking with you about her murder. Not anyone's."

Peter cursed under his breath, muttering, "He's toying with me, with us." He pawed at his hair, mussing it, as he gathered his thoughts.

He would need to go over it all. Read all the notes he had, and get the three of them back on the same page. Walking to the wall, he opened the panel into the time travel room. "I have copies of my notes in here. Please give me a moment."

Peter surveyed the filing cabinets in his time travel room. He unlocked and pulled open the drawer containing his most recent files, the ones he'd been reviewing overnight. Noticing a folder on top of the cabinet, he flipped through its contents, and realized there had been *five* women murdered. Somehow, as the timeline had changed while he slept, the murderer had removed the latest murders from the Weathers' memories; but on some other night — it must have been Friday — Roman had erased another murder, and all three of them had lost memories of it. The one Peter didn't recall had happened in New Mexico.

Suddenly, Peter fully understood Carrie's spells of anxiety. *To lose one's memory and then become aware of its loss, is unnerving*, he thought. He wondered what else had been corrected that he hadn't noticed. *Is that how he got the drop on me at the pond?* The thought gave him some relief. He hadn't been slipping. With much work to be done, he'd leave that to think about another time.

He stepped up to the threshold of the time travel room where the panel stood open. The Weathers still sat in his office chairs. "I'll read my notes from in here, and try to bring your memories up to mine. And refresh mine, to be honest. Looks like I've forgotten one of the victims myself."

When Mig looked puzzled, Peter said, "It's clear to me you've lost your memories, and I've lost some of mine, because this other time traveler is playing with us. He's undone his murders, except for Silvia Andrews."

This time, it was Mig who swore under his breath.

Peter shook his head. "This is good. This is actually good. Now we can stop him with only one woman dead at his hands. He's done some of our work for us. We have a unique moment, I think. We can stop him before he goes after anyone else."

"I get it. I think Carrie does, too. It's just a little hard right now, learning somebody wiped our minds."

"You're right," Peter said, tapping his hand on the threshold. "When we're all up-to-speed again, we can set a plan to stop him, and soon. We won't give him another chance to mess with us."

Peter shuffled through his notes relating to each murder, including information on Mig and Carrie's actions with him, which were actions, and conversations, that they now had never experienced. Carrie wrote down each name, address, and date as Peter yelled it out to her from his secret room.

With Mig and Carrie convinced — that four murders had happened and then been *corrected* somehow — Peter took Carrie's list and added notes next to each woman's name, then handed it back to her. "Would you mind researching where these not-murdered women are now? I think we'll find these women alive and well."

"I didn't bring my laptop. Let me run home for it, and if it's okay with you I'll set up in your kitchen and work on this."

"No problem," Peter said. "I think it will take me a while to reconstruct our map, and bring you both up-to-speed." He tacked a map on the wall, then wrote on a piece of paper and hung it next to the map.

He looked angry for a moment, then added, "And I'll make a copy of the map to put in the time travel room for safekeeping. I don't want us to go through this again."

"Okay, I'll be back soon. You two have fun," Carrie teased. Then, she noticed the paper Peter had tacked up on the wall.

Peter had written the names of the victims on a piece of paper — the same names he'd given her. Carrie stared at the list. The four NC victims names were in one column, with Angie by herself under the heading, "New Mexico." Carrie stood in front of the list, transfixed.

"What's up?" Mig asked. "Did you find something?"

Carrie picked up a pen and began drawing slowly on the paper. When she set down the pen, Mig and Peter stepped closer.

She had circled the first letters of the NC women's first and last names: Silvia Andrews, Valerie Edmonds, Tamsin Hawthorne, and Emma Morrison.

Their initials spelled, SAVE THEM.

Without commenting, Carrie left the men standing, staring at the list on the wall, promising she'd be back soon.

"I'm sick of this cat and mouse game," Peter said, hitting the wall with his fist.

Three hours later, Carrie yelled down to Peter's office, asking the men to come and see what she'd found. She led them through a dozen tabs open in her browser, showing each woman, posts each had made to social media, and a timeline of each woman's movements made from their online shares.

When Carrie finished going over her findings, Peter began pacing. "They are all okay. They weren't murdered. That's good. I'm glad. But, I know that they had been and we did not correct the timeline to save them. If our murderer is a time traveler, we need to find him soon. I doubt he'll leave his body count at one for very long."

Mig cleared his throat. "Um, could your grandfather have corrected all this, and a regular person is the murderer?"

"No," Peter said, running his hand through his hair. "I need you two to know. The more we discover, the more I believe I'm correct that the killer is Roman, and I'm done underestimating him."

I've underestimated myself, too, Peter thought. *I'm not slowing down from age. We've been chasing a killer who could move through time. Now that I know, I can find a way to beat him.*

Peter dove in. It was far past time. "Now that we're all on the same page, I need to talk with you about something else. I'm taking a very special trip. I have to find out more about Roman, and specifically about stopping time travelers. I'd like you two to join me.

"I'm sure you remember the note and map my Grampa left for me. Well, I think I need to go. I want to see this place out in New Mexico, and find out more about Roman's family, my family, and see if there's anything that can help me... us... determine why Roman is toying with us. Plus, I have questions about how to stop him and I need to get answers. I want you two to go with me, and as soon as possible."

Mig looked at him, "You want us to go with you to New Mexico?"

Peter glanced at Mig and laughed, "Yes, I do. But, it would be to New Mexico a long time ago. I'd like you both to travel back with me over a hundred years. It's further than I've been, and I don't know what I'll find, but I would like you to learn what I learn. I'd appreciate it if you are there to see what I see. You two might even notice things that I don't. You saw my grandfather's note. So, you know as much as I do about going back to the eighteen-hundreds."

Carrie sat quietly for a while, then asked Peter, "Is there any danger in this? I mean, what do you expect it'll be like there? What year are we talking about?"

Peter let out a loud "Ha," then shook his head. "I don't know. I can't guarantee there won't be danger. We'll be going back to 1898 and that was a rough time in the west." Peter grew serious, "We'll follow the map to my family, which should mean we can be 'among friends,' as people say. I don't know enough to say what the trip will be like. And, not to frighten you, but it is many years back, and my experience with such a trip is nonexistent."

"What do you expect to find out then that can help stop Roman now?" Mig asked.

"What I do know is that when I sent Grampa a message about Roman, he told me to go there. I have to believe there's something for me to learn, or he wouldn't have pointed me in that direction, in that context. It won't delay us much, as we'll return the morning after we leave, even if we stay back there several days."

"We'll go," Carrie blurted, surprising them both.

Mig hesitated, and asked, "Peter, when things are corrected with these killings, would you do me a favor? I'd like to go back in time and meet my grandparents. My mom was orphaned young, so I never met them. I'd like the chance to."

"Sounds like a good idea. We'll find a time to do it in the near future.

"We'll leave for old New Mexico tomorrow: Sunday evening. We'll be back with just enough time to work in whatever details I can pick up from this Adell person, and have our plan set for when Roman arrives Monday night for us to deal with him."

After Carrie extracted a promise from Peter that the visit to long-ago New Mexico wouldn't cause ripples that put the Weathers children at risk, they parted company for the night.

***

Late that evening, Peter scribbled notes across a typed page. It was a script he'd prepared, for a call he planned to make to Roman.

When he finished, he sat tall in his desk chair and carefully rehearsed it. It was mostly lies, and he wanted to get it right. It was an important role he was about to play, thankfully by phone where Roman couldn't read his body language.

This first part of Peter's plan was to agree to help Roman with his children, though he had no intention of doing anything, and knew the children were nonexistent. He did, however, need to lure Roman to his house at a predetermined time.

He made the call. Peter went through his script, telling Roman he was going to help him. He'd predicted Roman's responses fairly well, and by the end Roman thanked him and promised he'd be there at the agreed upon date, Monday, at 10 P.M.

Peter hung up the phone and pulled several pages from his desk. He reviewed his rough plan to stop Roman. Peter still held out hope he could stop Roman without killing him. But, he'd do what had to be done.

The plan was close to useless, he knew. But his next step would help him to flesh out a good plan. The next step was to follow his Grampa's instructions and travel to the past.

After that, Peter hoped, he would know enough to confirm if the murder was an ordinary man or Roman, and if Roman, he'd have to learn how to stop him.

Before he went to bed, Peter placed a longer-than-usual classified ad in the Denver newspaper. It let his Grampa know he was going to see Adell, he'd taken on two apprentices, and he'd be meeting Roman again — including the place, date, and time of the meeting.

26 – Hello, 1898

As she dressed for the trip, Mig commented to Carrie that she seemed calm. She shrugged and said, "When else will I have a chance to see the eighteen hundreds?"

They'd locked up their house, and told the kids they were going away for a few days on a mini-vacation. Even though the plan was to come back to what would be the following morning, Carrie had insisted on the ruse, wanted to be sure that if they for some reason ended up botching their return from a hundred years ago, the kids wouldn't worry right away. If all went well, they'd be "back" tomorrow and just tell the kids they decided not to go on a trip.

"Or," Mig suggested, "We could take a trip on our own. I think we're gonna need a break after this." He winked at Carrie, and she sighed.

"Sounds good to me," she said, and kissed him.

Loading their car, they drove to Peter's house. Mig and Carrie arrived just in time for a last, fast, modern cup of coffee. As Peter led them into the kitchen, Carrie saw he was dressed simply, as he had asked them to be. All were in jeans and heavy cotton shirts with long sleeves — the closest they had to nineteenth century, simpler clothing.

They had barely sipped their drinks when a more-agitated -than-normal Peter said, "Let's go."

They dragged their packs downstairs to the office. Each had a backpack, and on Peter's suggestion all of their bags were canvas. Not old-fashioned, but at least not made of material that would make them stand out, as the bright-and-shiny fabrics of their time wouldn't be recognized in the time to which they'd be traveling.

After Carrie made a quick trip to the bathroom, "while running water and toilet paper are still available," she and Mig joined Peter in the time travel room. Uncharacteristically, he asked them to grab his hands. They did, and Mig grabbed Carrie's free hand.

Peter chuckled, "We don't actually have to hold hands. But, good to know you'll follow my instructions."

He chortled as they released his hands. "You can't fault a teacher for making a little joke, to relieve the tension and all. Calm down so we can all concentrate. I'll do the work, and we'll be targeting a spot a little way away from the X on my grandfather's map, at 10 A.M. on his birthday in 1898."

Mig was still holding Carrie's hand and gave it a squeeze. She squeezed back, laughing lightly. *'Socially awkward' doesn't quite cut it*, she thought; one of Mig's comments years ago when they'd first met the odd time traveler.

Peter took a deep breath, closing his eyes. Mig and Carrie followed his example and closed theirs, and Peter let out a long, slow breath. Carrie felt the jump as before, and Peter said, "Okay, we're here."

Carrie opened her eyes and looked around. "Wow!" she exclaimed, seeing they were no longer in the little room, but standing together in a vast forest. The trees seemed to go on forever in every direction.

"The air smells different," Mig said, turning around and looking in all directions. He stopped spinning and took several deep breaths, exhaling exaggeratedly.

Carrie follow suit. *Very different*, she thought. Woodsy smells, a dampness, and not subtle. It took her a moment before she realized it was the *missing* smells that made the smells of the forest so strong. The natural scents weren't buried under smoke, car exhaust, fast food oils, and the generalized "downtown" smells to which they were accustomed. "Clean."

"Clean. That's a good word," Peter said. He was giving off his twitchy, Spiky Hair Guy nervousness. It started making Carrie nervous, so she distracted herself by surveying the amazing, overgrown, undeveloped terrain around them.

"We need to walk a quarter-mile in that direction," Peter said, pointing.

"Let's go." Mig started walking in the direction Peter had indicated. It was downhill for now, Carrie was glad to see. There was little underbrush, yet she stumbled several times as she followed the two men, wishing she'd worn sneakers instead of her bulky hiking boots.

Carrie could hear Mig and Peter talking back-and-forth as she brought up the rear. After about ten minutes, they reached the valley floor and Carrie caught up to them. Peter pointed across the valley. "There it is," he said chipperly.

She saw an amazed look on Mig's face and stepped forward to see where Peter was pointing. She sucked in a breath and held it, then rubbed her eyes and looked again.

Up the valley was a round building, flat upon the ground, grass-roofed, and half as long as a football field. Tall trees ringed it, hiding it from view from anyone on the surrounding hilltops. A figure could be seen moving near it. "I guess that will be my family," Peter said. "Let me lead, and let's hope I look familiar enough that they'll welcome us."

They walked the rest of the distance with Peter in front, Mig and Carrie staying slightly behind, holding hands.

The complex centered around the large building. When they reached its edge, Mig ran his hand along the wall. "Interesting."

"It looks old," Carrie added, putting her hand against it.

They were greeted by a young woman holding a basket of vegetables, her brown hair tucked under a floppy straw hat, curly strands escaping and revealing its length. She said,

"Hola," with a suspicion-tinged tone before asking who they were in Spanish, then in English.

Peter bowed for some reason, then responded, "Me llamo Peter. My name is Peter." He pointed to and named Carrie, who bowed where she was, and pointed to and named Mig last. Mig extended his hand.

The woman shook the offered hand, then returned her gaze to Peter. In English, Peter asked, "What is your name?"

"Adell," she said, warily, "What brings you three here, and on this day?"

Peter stepped forward, "I was told I could find my family here."

Adell squinted at Peter, then pursed her lips. "What is your family name? I know everyone for many miles around." She waved her free hand across the view.

"I am Peter Horacio Braggin," he told her.

She looked Peter up and down. "The Horacios are *my* family. I am Adell Horacio Jones. I don't know you."

Peter reached into his backpack and pulled out the photograph of his grandfather his mother, and his great-grandfather. He handed it to Adell, who set down her basket and took it in both hands.

She looked at it, turning it over in her hand. "What is this? How can this be?"

Peter realized too late that she wouldn't have seen a 1950s photograph before, maybe never seen any photograph as she lived so remotely. *Another mistake in my planning*, he thought. "That's a photograph of my, um, relatives. Do you know them?"

"I know of him," she pointed at Peter's great-grandfather, Manuel. Her eyes shifted, giving the impression she was holding something back. Then, she nodded hard, as if affirming something to herself. "He is Manuel, but he looks older in this." She held the photo out to Peter, pinching it by the edge, as if afraid of it.

Peter took the photograph back. He looked embarrassed as he replaced it in his backpack.

Mig jumped in, "Is there somewhere you would let us set down our packs so you and Peter can talk, Ma'am?"

Adell looked at Mig, then did a double take. She looked him up and down, her eyes widening.

After a moment, she addressed Peter again, "Come with me, travelers." She whirled and walked toward a rough door leading into the rounded house. They followed behind her in a line, Carrie picking up Adell's forgotten basket as she walked.

She led them to a door along the side of the building. She swung it open and motioned for them to come inside. Peter took the door and held it open for Mig, who held it for Carrie, who stepped tentatively through the crude wooden doorway and allowed the door to swing shut behind her.

The Weathers stood just inside, looking around in wonder. "Pretty interesting place," Mig said in a low voice.

Carrie clutched Mig's arm and whispered, "What was that movie where the time travelers were killed for being too strange? Oh, wait, it wasn't in a *movie*. That's *our lives right now*." Mig looked horrified for a moment, then Carrie grinned, and he sighed, realizing she was joking. He gave her shoulder a light squeeze.

"Very funny," he said.

"Come," Adell's voice boomed across the room, an ornately carved kitchen complete with a wood stove at least ten feet long. She motioned furtively to them, pointed Peter to a chair, then pushed them toward two other chairs. They all sat dutifully.

She brought out bread and vegetables, along with slices of cold meat. What kind of meat, Carrie couldn't tell.

As they ate, Adell asked Peter no questions, but talked much. She spoke of her parents and grandparents. Carrie noticed Mig's eyes glazing over, and she wondered if his thoughts were on his mother again.

Adell talked about her home — the rounded shape and how it protected them from the winds, keeping the inside warm year-round. She even talked about the surrounding gardens, and how they grew enough to store food through the winters when fewer things grew.

Finally, she asked Peter, "Why are you traveling to here?"

Peter cleared his throat, then answered, "My friends and I have come from far, traveling here to learn more about the Horacios."

Not much of an answer, but true, Mig thought.

Adell looks sideways at Peter. She seemed to be considering what he'd said. "You've picked a good day to come. I have been expecting Manuel and his wife Flora to return home for a month. I don't know what's delayed them, but I'm hoping they will arrive today." She looked at each of her visitors. "I believe your arrival is a sign we will see them today. This is an important date to which you have come, yes?"

"Yes, it is," Peter said.

Carrie was awed by the not-specifically-stating-it way that Adell made them aware she knew they were time travelers.

"Okay. Good." Adell nodded her head once. She placed a plate of bread and a stiff-looking cheese on the table. "You eat, then you rest, or go outside but stay close. We'll talk later."

The rest of the afternoon, Peter, Mig, and Carrie wandered the compound. They were allowed in all areas of the structure and around the gardens. Adell seemed to take joy in describing each garden as she saw them approach it. She grew a variety of vegetables and beans, along with medicinal herbs, and something Mig pointed out to Carrie that he was sure was marijuana.

"No corn or wheat?" Carrie asked at one point. She had eaten the bread they'd been given, and knew Adell must have some grain.

"I trade with my cousin," she said, pointing toward a hill. "He lives over there. He talks too much, so you won't be going to visit."

A field was visible in the distance, wrapping across a hilltop, though Carrie saw no buildings. Then, she realized that a large rock poking up from the center of the field was not a rock, but another round structure, much smaller than Adell's.

She prodded Mig, pointing toward it. Mig leaned toward her and whispered, "We should have brought a camera or our phones, even though Peter said not to."

As night fell, they gathered inside the structure. Adell refused Carrie's and Mig's offers to help with the food, though she thrust a bowl of carrots and a small knife in Peter's hands, and asked him to cut the carrots for their meal.

Just as she said the meal was ready, the outer door opened. Adell greeted the newcomers warmly. "Hola!" she said as she hugged a tall, dust-covered man and a very pregnant, tired woman. Another man, older, came in after them with a small child of about a year and a half. Adell ran to the older man and hugged him, kissing the child, "Husband, welcome back. Hello, my Adelina."

"Hola," the pregnant woman panted. "Adell, the baby is coming."

Adell folded the woman in her arms, "I made up a room for you to be comfortable. Walk with me." Adell turned and glowered at the dusty man as she led the woman from the room. "Heat water, Manuel. Your baby is coming." Adell yelled over her shoulder, "Carrie, you follow me. You help."

Carrie was aghast. Mig must have seen the terror in her eyes. He put his hand on her back and pushed her gently in the direction Adell had gone, "You can do it. It'll be okay."

Carrie gaped at Mig. Then, she nodded meekly. "I'll do what I can, I guess," her voice shaking.

Mig watched her go, then looked at Peter. "We should have brought my friend Dr. Lopez," Peter said seriously. Then Peter introduced himself to the woman's husband, who said he was Manuel Horacio, and his wife's name was Flora. Mig stood and shook the man's hand, introducing himself and Carrie. Adell's husband set Adelina on the floor, and as she toddled off across the kitchen, he introduced himself. "I'm Adam Jones. Welcome to our home."

Adam walked to the stove, cursing as he hunted for a pot. Peter and Mig helped him find an empty one, and he poured water from a jug into it.

Despite the advanced look of Adell's home from the outside, the kitchen was rustic and, to Mig, old-fashioned. They sorted out what Adell needed for the baby's delivery, while Manuel stood staring down the hall, mercilessly twisting his dusty hat with his hands.

When it was ready, Adam sent Peter down the hall with the pot of hot water for Adell. As he entered the room, with Mig following tentatively behind him, they saw that the baby was already born. Peter set the pot down near Adell. She shot the men a hard stare, then dipped the edge of a rag into the water, shook it to cool it, and began gently washing the baby's face. After long minutes of cleaning and cooing, she wrapped the baby — a boy — in a clean cloth and held him out to Peter. Seeing him hesitate, she instead passed the newborn over to Mig.

"Take him and go while your vieja and I care for Flora."

Carrie's eyes were wide, her skin tinted slightly green. Mig winked at her, then took the baby and returned to the kitchen. He heard Adell shooing Peter out of the room too, shutting the door after him, and he followed Mig.

In the kitchen, Manuel scooped the baby from Mig's arms. He opened the cloth and grinned when he saw it was a boy. He patted the baby, then handed it back to Mig and turned to watch down the hall, apparently waiting for Adell to emerge with news of his wife.

Mig held the baby low so little Adelina could see her newborn cousin. She peeked, and then ran to hug her daddy's leg. Adam smiled at his daughter and patted her head. Unsure what else to do, Mig stood with the baby, swaying slightly as if rocking it.

Peter approached, gawking. "Hello, Grampa Alfonso. Happy birthday." Peter looked as if he was about to cry.

"Grampa?" questioned Manuel. "Then you *are* one of us. From when have you traveled, Peter Braggin?"

Peter was about to answer when Carrie appeared, wiping her hands on a dampened cloth. She put her arm around Mig as she looked at the new little boy. "Wow," she said. Mig kissed her on the forehead.

Carrie turned toward Manuel. "Adell said to tell you your wife is fine, and you can go in now."

Manuel raced down the hall into the back room, slamming the door behind him in his haste. Adam laughed, his daughter watched him for a moment, a puzzled look on her face, then laughed with him.

Adell returned to the kitchen an hour later. She waved toward a doorway, then nudged Peter on the arm. "There is a large room on the other side of the house, far from the new baby and sleeping mama. You three maybe saw it when you were walking around the house today? Sleep there. I've left you some thick blankets. Okay?" Then she bustled to the stove, turning her back to them.

Peter picked up his pack. Mig and Carrie grabbed theirs, and followed Peter into the large room Adell had indicated. Peter waited to see where Mig and Carrie dropped their packs, then took his own into the furthest corner from them.

He grabbed one of the blankets Adell had set out, and tucked up in the corner, using his pack as an awkward pillow.

"Well, at least this is more comfortable than the floor of my time travel room. Good night." He turned and faced the wall.

Mig and Carrie could hear him breathing deeply, fast asleep, even before they spread their own blankets on the floor.

After a kiss, both settled onto the floor, struggled a little with the short, itchy coverings, and soon fell asleep.

27 – Records Room

In the middle of the night, with the others slept, Adell shook Peter awake. Shushing him, she motioned for him to follow her and tip-toed from the room. Peter tossed his blanket aside and, creaking slightly, pulled himself upright and followed her.

Adell led Peter into a room across the hall from the one where Flora had earlier given birth.

Adell moved a small, crate-like furnishing — Adelina's version of a crib, Peter guessed — away from the rear wall. Stepping back, Adell pressed against the wall with her palm, and it swung open revealing another room. She walked inside. Peter followed, and saw the room was at least fifty feet long, and chock-full of shelves and tables. Books were everywhere.

She picked up an oversized journal and flipped it open. The pages were covered with drawings and handwritten notes, held together by stitching at one edge. She held it up, pointing to a page that listed Manuel and Flora, and the generations before them. She had already written in the child, whose name was to be Alfonso Manuel Horacio — Peter's grandfather. He touched the page.

"Anything you wish to know of our family, I think you can find in here," she said. "Start with this book, and you're welcome to all the others. Please be quiet, so the new mama may rest. Adelina is with us, so you won't be disturbed."

Peter scanned the shelves and piles of books. Many were hand bound and labeled with names; these he guessed were journals. What he needed to know about the family, and especially Roman's family, was in here and it would take hours to find it.

Adell spoke in a low voice. "My father was Mountain Horacio, named so by his father who was one of the original sojourners — which is what they were called. Now we in the family say *travelers*. I've heard *you* say travelers, so you know that term. There were four sojourners at the start, which the books will tell you if you go through them all. To save you time, I share what my father told me. He told me his father was a sojourner who took the name Uno — which, of course, means *one*," she laughed. "It took them two generations before the family did a good job at naming their children.

"The other three sojourners were named, as you might guess, Dos, Tres, and Cuatro, though eventually they found better names to call themselves. Poor Cuatro died soon after they arrived, though, which was 1838." She flipped through a large book, then set it on a table in front of Peter.

"Arrived from where?" Peter asked.

Peter waited tensely for Adell to respond to the question. She only waved her hand and said, "No importa. It does not matter."

Peter shifted his weight back on his heels, his face showing his disappointment.

Adell continued, "Each of these ancestors could do what you have done, Peter. What I have done. They could go backward through time, and to other places, and make things different there."

"My grandfather Alfonso called his changes 'corrections.'

She pursed her lips and stared coldly at him. After a brief silence, Adell asked, "What have you come to *correct* here, Peter?"

Peter smiled, holding up his hand, palm toward her. "Adell, I am here to change nothing. I've only come to learn."

Adell's face relaxed, and her eyes closed briefly and re-opened. "Good. By coming here, you know you might change things you didn't mean to change. I will be careful. I will not let this change our family's future. When you and your companions leave, we will all vow to never speak of your visit. Alfonso will never be told. It will be best."

She closed the book and handed it to Peter. "Use this as you can, and any of the books and papers in this room. And tomorrow after the sun sets, you can ask me more, and I'll tell you more. But, I'm tired."

"I have one question, if you could please tell me where I would find information on anyone named Vasquez."

Adell wrinkled her nose as if she'd smelled something rotten. She stepped around Peter and grabbed a hand-stitched book with rough-cut pages. "Here is what you need to know." Under her breath, she swore in Spanish — a choice phrase Peter had heard his grandfather use on rare occasions. She pushed the book roughly into Peter's hands. "Fire gave himself that name, Vasquez, and said it was the name of a trader he knew. More likely, he murdered a Vasquez and stole their name. Fire threw away the Horacio name, and I am happy the name separated his kin from the rest of us. It soiled the name." She snorted in disgust.

Adell stepped out through the doorway with a flourish. "Good night. Or, morning," she said, closing the broad door behind her, leaving Peter alone in the book room.

Nearby, Flora, Manuel, and baby Alfonso slept, and Peter could hear Manuel's snores through the wall. Peter settled the heavy book onto a table and sat carefully, quietly, onto a chair. He began reading.

Carrie awoke first the next morning. It was so quiet. No refrigerator humming, no traffic sounds. As sun streamed in the window, she heard murmuring from the kitchen. She kept still, listening to the birds singing outside for a time; then, she realized Mig was standing at the window.

"Good morning," she said.

"Good morning, sweetheart," he responded in a whisper.

She peered toward the opposite corner. Peter was gone and the blanket next to his pack.

She stood, straightening her slept-in clothes and doing her best to un-muss her hair, while she noticed Mig's looked as perfect as ever.

Carrie folded her blankets and pushed them against the wall, alongside Mig's already folded bedding. She joined him at the window, giving him the first kiss of the day.

"What do you think of this?" asked Mig, tapping his knuckles against the outer wall. It made a metallic tinging sound.

"Are those metal walls?" she asked, incredulously.

"Yep." Changing the subject, Mig said, "I hear talking in the kitchen. Are you hungry?"

Carrie rubbed her stomach and nodded. "Definitely. I hadn't realized that snacking was a modern thing. Meals here... now... seem far apart."

Mig turned from the window and together they headed for the kitchen. "True. We better not miss our chance to eat. C'mon, wife. Let's go find out what coffee tasted like in 1898."

They shuffled into the kitchen to check out the coffee situation. Adell invited them to sit, then took a seat by Carrie. "No one outside the family has been taught our ways before. I am glad Peter has chosen to pass this on to you. The family was small to start with, and from what Peter has said, it doesn't grow much in the coming hundred years." Adell shrugged.

Carrie asked, "Are there things we can't learn, or can't do, because we aren't blood relatives?"

Adell cocked her head, "Peter says you have been helping him. I know of no one outside of our family who had been told this, or could move through time."

"Mig learned how. I just came along with him and Peter," Carrie said with a shrug.

"They've learned quickly," Peter said, entering the kitchen. He looked disheveled and his eyes were red. "And I believe they have the hearts to use it wisely."

Adell looked at Peter, her head cocked to the side again. "Have you told them also how to explore the minds of others? To search for another's intentions?"

Carrie's mouth dropped open. She looked at Mig, and he at her, surprise in their eyes. They both turned and looked at Peter. Carrie saw the same surprised look on Peter's face.

After a moment's hesitation, Peter asked Adell, "We can do what now?"

Adell laughed, "Surely you realized you could tell what is in a person's mind, Peter."

"Peter?" Mig asked. "Something you want to tell us?"

Peter looked agape at Adell, Mig, Carrie, and back at Adell. Defensively, he said, "I have a knack for figuring people out. I didn't... I mean, I just thought I was good at reading people, not reading their *minds*!"

Adell laughed and laughed.

"Wow," Carrie said, mentally reviewing previous conversations with Peter. Often, he'd seemed to say what she was thinking. Had he really known her thoughts?

"Do not worry, Carrie. He cannot know all that you think while you are with Mig. We travelers keep our thoughts protected, and our mate's." Adell suppressed another laugh and wiped water from her eyes.

"But--" Peter started.

Adell waved Peter off. "There is more to the Horacio family than traveling through time. It's how we are."

Soon after, Adell's husband Adam invited the three travelers to come fishing with him. "There are many of us to feed today, and I'd appreciate help," Adam said, handing a long pole to Mig.

"Good," Adell said. "Put them to work! We have work to do here and I do not want them under our feet."

"Sure," Mig said. What are we catching?"

"Fish," Adam said simply, and began walking.

Waving good-bye to Carrie — whose help, according to Adell, would be better in the garden than fishing — Mig followed Adam and Peter away from the compound.

That evening after a dinner of fish with vegetables, Mig and Carrie sat in their room, speaking in low voices. Mig shared with Carrie his fishing adventure, starting with the twenty-minute walk to a large, clear lake, and culminating in the dozen large fish they'd eaten for dinner.

After his tale was told, she filled him in on her gardening and chores, concluding with how thankful she was that they had things like a dishwasher, washing machine, and rototiller back in their own time.

Exhausted by the day's activities, she soon fell asleep in his arms.

After a few hours sleep, Peter returned to the records room to research Roman and other family members. He'd slept little since arriving, knowing that the more he learned of the family, the better his chances to outwit Roman.

Peter absorbed details of the original sojourners, their surviving children, and found a notebook describing the very same methods his own Grampa had taught him. He almost sidetracked himself when he found several loose pages describing the behavior of wolves and their apparent attraction to those who had recently traveled through time.

A tied stack of papers caught his eye. Stepping around a book-laden table, he reached down and retrieved the small stack. A few minutes of reading, and he knew this was what he had been seeking.

The writings were unsigned, but obviously written by a time traveler with a good grasp of English. Page-after-page described issues with Fire — sometimes as Horacio and on later dates Vasquez — and his kin. Twice he was referred to as Fuego, in narratives describing time changes he had made that were denounced by the writer.

It became apparent to Peter that Fire had cut a swath through time full of evil deeds, murders, and — starting when he was young — childish and harmful pranks on locals and wanderers alike. Even worse, Fire's referenced *wife*, it seemed, had been more victim than partner, according to two newspaper clippings Peter found tucked in the hand-written stack. *The old-time equivalent of a police blotter*, he thought.

At the bottom of the stack, a different writer had taken over. These pages listed terrible deeds by Fire's children, with a denouncement of them as untrustworthy in word and deed. The final page described the disappearance of Fire's son, Samuel Vasquez, in 1896 after his kidnapping of a young woman.

Since Adell did not know of Roman, as they were visiting around the year he would have been born, Peter made the assumption that Samuel may have done more than just kidnap the woman; he may have impregnated her.

The more Peter read, the more it confirmed what he feared — that Roman was not just the liar Peter believed him to be, but he had come from a long line of men who had chosen to harm women. Peter thought of how this contrasted to how he was taught to help others and to be kind, from the time he was small. His mother and grandparents taught him to respect time travel and use it to make a positive impact. Meanwhile, Roman's family seemed to live for themselves, willing to harm others when it suited them. Peter wondered if the Vasquez clan had also used time travel to further exploit others.

He leaned back and thought over what he'd learned in the past two nights from Adell's books. After lengthy writing into his own notebook, he gave in to the urge to gather as much family information as he could, and used his cell phone's camera to take photos of many pages — including the pages on wolves.

He slid his cell phone into his pocket in case one of the present-day people walked in. Adell had been clear she did not want knowledge of his time. Plus, he didn't want to run the battery down with no outlets available. Not to mention he'd hidden his phone from Mig and Carrie, and the last thing he needed was for them to find out he was taking photos when he'd requested they not pack any technology.

Putting the books back in place, leaving the room as he found it, he read the pages on Roman's family one more time. He thought, *I'm careful with time travel because my Grampa taught me so. If Roman's ancestors lived for their own enjoyment, and to torture others, maybe this is all Roman was taught. Maybe that's why he traveled to play games with me.*

"It all fits," he said aloud, then cringed as the baby on the other side of the wall let out a wail.

Unable to tell inside the records room if it was morning yet, Peter guessed it was when he smelled food. He rubbed his eyes, and decided to head into the kitchen, taking his notebook with him.

Everyone was already digging into breakfast, Peter accepted a plate from Adell and sat down.

As she ate her last bites of egg, Carrie noticed Adell staring at Mig. He must have seen her, too, as he paused with a piece of homemade bread halfway to his mouth. Adell smiled, then turned to Peter, and asked, "Did you happen across the name Miguel in your research?" She motioned toward Peter's notebook. A slight smile tickled at the corner of her mouth.

Peter didn't look up from his plate, and didn't notice Mig's sudden, frozen appearance. "No, I don't think so. At least, not yet. Is that an ancestor of yours or mine?"

In the silence that followed, Peter continued eating. Carrie looked from Mig to Adell and back. Mig placed the bread in his mouth and chewed slowly, looking at the women, his expression as full of puzzlement as Carrie felt.

Adell stood abruptly and left the room, returning a few minutes later with what looked to Carrie like a hand-sewn book, many pages thick. Peter wiped his mouth and leaned back. "What's that?" He did a double take as he noticed Mig's expression for the first time.

"This one is about my family," Adell said, tapping one finger on the tanned leather cover.

She gently turned its pages, stopping close to the back.

"Adam, mi esposo. You fished with him and spent time with him. His father is Miguel. Adam, he is no traveler, but I know already our children will be. Adelina shows promise, and more will come. Even I don't know for sure when. Mi Adam will return for dinner tonight and you must..." She trailed off, lovingly running her fingers down the page.

"Is something wrong?" Carrie asked. She thought she saw tears in Adell's eyes, but Adell didn't look sad. At least, not to Carrie's mind. If Carrie had to guess, Adell's tears were joyful.

Adell shook her head at Carrie's question, then focused on Mig. "You are friends of Peter's for a long time?"

In her peripheral vision, she saw that Peter had risen, walking around the table to look at the open pages in front of Adell. She could hear Mig ripping bread, and shifted to look at him.

Peter shook his head. "Well, not a long time. For a while now, and we met years ago."

"How many years ago, Mig Weathers?" she asked sharply.

Before Mig could respond, Peter answered, "Just a few years. Why?"

"Did you meet traveling through time, Peter?"

"No." Peter looked at her as if she were mad. "I am the one who travels. I met them in my time. They weren't time travelers until I taught them. Well, Mig can do what I can, and Carrie helps us. What's going on?"

Adell folded her arms on top of the book and leaned toward Mig. "Who is your family? Your mother? Your father?"

Mig coughed, choking for a moment on the bite he'd taken before swallowing in what Carrie thought looked like a painful way. Then he said, "Carl and Lina Weathers."

"And their parents?"

"My dad's parents, the Weathers, lived in the UK. I only met them once before they passed. My mom Lina was adopted when she was eight and given the name Lina Gonzalez. Her adoptive parents were--"

Adell cut him off with a wave. "Not them. What were Lina's *parents'* names?"

"What are you--" Peter started, but Adell shushed him savagely.

Carrie stared at Mig. She could feel the tension rising in the room. Leaning, Carrie tried to read the pages open in front of Adell, but the woman's arms were still covering the book.

"Where did your mother get your name, Miguel? Did she ever say if yours was a family name?" She waved her hand in the air, her voice getting louder. "Did she pull it from a hat? Name you for a neighbor? *Where*?"

The hair stood up on the back of Carrie's neck. She pushed her chair backward, away from all of them, without realizing she'd done so. Peter, who was standing still, stared at Mig.

She saw Mig's hand clench in a fist, his remaining bread squashing inside it. "My mom... She was eight when her parents died in a car crash. Mom said she'd named me after her biological father. Mom's parents were Miguel and Anna Jones." His face blanched as he heard himself say *Jones*.

Mig swore under his breath, his eyes wide with surprise.

Adell tapped her hand on the table in the way Carrie had seen Peter tap things when one of them finally grasped a point he had been trying to make.

Adell leaned back and pointed at the open page in front of her. "Adam's father Miguel is where the name comes from. Miguel died before Adam's birth. His mother, Chastity Jones, was not married to Miguel, and named the child Adam Jones, rather than name him for his dead father. She told Adam nothing of Miguel's family.

"When Adam and I have a son, we plan to name him Miguel to reclaim the family name. Our son is to be your grandfather." She tapped the page several more times, and Carrie got a glimpse of a hand-drawn family tree with Adam and Adell's names in the center.

"But," Carrie objected, "Jones is a common name in our time. The name Miguel is common. Why would you think--"

Adell slapped the page and answered Carrie in a much louder voice than Carrie thought necessary. "I don't *think it* because of the names. I ask the names, because I see your husband's eyes are my husband's eyes, your husband Mig's chin is my chin." She punctuated this by raising her chin and placing her finger on it. "I know your Mig is of my family to come. I'm right about this." She waggled her finger at Carrie, then at Mig. "So, I know you are a relative. You would know it, Miguel Weathers, if you were paying attention."

She handed the old book to Carrie. "I think you and Mig should read of my family."

Carrie scanned the page, Peter reading over her shoulder. This time, it was Peter who swore under his breath. Adell nudged him hard on the leg and he stopped.

Adell nodded her head in self-satisfaction, took the book away from Carrie, and handed it to Mig. He dropped the crushed bread and took the book with both hands, standing and carefully balancing it as he scanned the page showing the family tree.

Adell began clearing the table as if nothing had happened.

At that moment, Adam came inside carrying firewood. "Mira!" Adell demanded, telling everyone to *look* in Spanish, and waving her hands toward her husband.

All eyes landed on Adam. "Qué?" he asked.

Adell gestured toward Mig, then back to her husband.

"Ah, you told them," Adam laughed, dropping the firewood by the stove.

Carrie looked back and forth from Adam's eyes to Mig's. *Adell is right. They have the same eyes.*

28 – Family

The rest of the day passed with Carrie and Peter staring too often at Mig and Adam.

In the hours between the jarring breakfast revelation and dinner, Adell allowed Mig and Carrie to explore the records room. "Mi familia," she said in a sing-song voice as she walked out the room's door.

During dinner, Carrie had to force herself to stop staring at Adam's eyes multiple times. The more she explored the man's face, the more resemblance she saw between him and Mig. She noticed Peter doing the same.

He and Adam peppered Mig with questions about his mother's family, what he remembered of her, and where she had lived before her parents were killed. Adam seemed less averse to learning about their time than Adell was.

At one point, Carrie turned to Peter and she said, "Man, am I relieved! No wonder I'm no good at jumping through time and Mig's a natural."

"Hey, you're part of the family, anyway," Mig said, teasing her.

"Yes," said Peter. "You absolutely are, cousins."

Adell snorted. "Mig has the blood of the sojourners so of course he can move through time."

"I didn't know. Sorry, Carrie," Peter said, "Thinking back on some of the things I've been teaching the two of you..."

"I'm totally fine with it," Carrie said with relish. "You two have the lead, and I will happily continue to serve as sidekick."

Adell nodded her assent. "Yes, you are one of us, as is my husband and others who have joined our family. Welcome to the family." Carrie and Mig both beamed.

"Oh, no!" Carrie said suddenly, dropping her spoon.

"What?" Mig grabbed her hand, concerned.

"Your daughter. Nicole is probably a time traveler like you! And the grand-kids! Oh, wow!"

Mig's golden skin turned as pale as it could, while Adell began laughing loudly, slapping the table repeatedly with her palm.

After dinner, and many minutes of cajoling, Adell and Adam agreed to stand with Peter, Mig, and Carrie for a photograph. Mig shot Peter a side glance when he saw Peter pull out his cell phone. "Leave our technology at home, right, Peter?"

Peter's face flushed. "Yeah, sorry. Technically not a rule, for future reference."

With a squirming Adelina in her arms, Adell smiled broadly as Manuel took the photo. It only took Peter explaining the cell phone twice before Manuel captured the perfect, multigenerational shot. Then, Peter took a photo of the Jones family, and individual shots of each of them around the kitchen.

Before they settled in for the night, Peter shared with Adell everything he knew about Roman and his family — up to and including their own time — and Adell filled in details that had not been in the book room. She also confirmed she was the writer of the most recent pages outlining Samuel's deeds and his recent disappearance with, as Adell described her, "a young girl he kidnapped."

***

Early on their fourth day in 1989, Mig and Carrie borrowed Peter's phone and ran off, planning to photograph the amazingly clean world they were visiting. Peter knew his battery would be toast, but he'd be home soon enough to charge it.

Peter stayed at the compound and walked with Adell, watching as she pulled tomatoes from loaded vines and dropped them into a wide basket.

"Adell, I have a problem," Peter said.

"Tell me."

"Back in our time, we have a man who is killing women. It's senseless. I want to stop him..." He paused.

"Stopping a man is a problem you can solve, especially with the help you have. Or, am I right you think this man is a time traveler?" Adell asked.

"You are. I do. I'm convinced it is Roman Vasquez."

Adell straightened, handing her laden basket to Peter. "Sojourners can be stopped only when they're dead. This you know. We cannot be held prisoner, which you also know, since we can travel away from any fortress you build."

"Yes," Peter said. "I would prefer not to kill him, if there is another way."

Adell looked Peter in the eye and crossed her arms over her chest. "If what you want is to confine him, I'm sorry but I know of no way to hold a traveler in a prison. Only death will stop him."

Peter sighed, then nodded his head. "I had hoped there was another option."

She looked at Peter, her expression softening. "We are blessed. It is unfortunate when one of our kin chooses to use traveling as a weapon against others."

Peter thought for a moment. "Adell, if he is a time traveler, and I must kill him, can I kill him in the past and leave him there?"

Adell stared at Peter as if he had two heads. "You know the answer. No traveler nor any person can be left in a time that is not their own."

"I didn't know--" Peter started.

"Yes, you know." She tapped her finger repeatedly on her forehead, demanding, "Think."

When Peter looked dumbfounded, and a smile teased at the edge of her mouth. "I will explain how you know."

She began walking again, picking from the garden and releasing fruits into the basket Peter carried. He kept up with her, waiting.

"You travel to other times, and always you return to your own time. It is easier to go home, because you are tied to your own time. You decide to go home, and you wake up in your nest. This--"

"My nest?" Peter asked, confused.

"The safe place where you sleep, from where you travel, and where you return and wake."

"My bedroom," Peter said. "I awake there. But I don't travel from there. My Grampa built a room from where we travel."

Adell looked amused by this. "You don't return to the place where you started your trip?"

"Well, near to it. Grampa's house has our time travel room downstairs, and we had bedrooms upstairs. We always woke up in our own rooms. I still do. Mig and Carrie, they live miles away but wake up in their beds at home. Anyone who stays in my time travel room while I go, they end up at their homes."

Adell chuckled. "That is interesting. It sounds like your nest is large, and their house is, too. I didn't know others could be returned to other places, nor that those who are not like us could travel or have a nest. I'd not tried other places, or taken other people, so you have taught me some things." She shrugged. "Your grandfather will be very smart when he grows up," she said, motioning toward her home and the sleeping baby within.

Adell stopped again, dropping a pepper into the basket, which was sagging a little from the weight of the harvest. "It is easy to return when you end your traveling, taking far less effort than when you go to another time. It is the same for all of us. If I was traveling and died, my body would return to the nest."

Peter nodded.

"If this man is a time traveler, and you kill him while he is traveling, then his body will go to his nest in his own time. If this man is not traveling and you kill him, he will stay where he falls dead. It does not matter if *you* are traveling. Do you understand?"

"I do," Peter said, "So, I can kill him at any point in time. His body may stay, or may disappear. I can plan around that."

"Good," Adell said. "You know when and where he will be to kill, so you will catch him. I have no doubt."

"Yes. And he'll stay where we kill him."

"He will. And, of course, his timeline will end there, and he won't live in your time anymore."

She dropped something Peter didn't recognize into the basket. "Once he's dead, leave him dead," Adell said, then chuckled.

"Yes, of course I will."

"Good," Adell said, still chuckling. "You don't want to do one of your *corrections* on a dead time traveler."

Peter paused. Mig was a time traveler. Peter had brought Mig back before he knew who Mig was. "Why not?"

Adell shot him a funny look. "You don't know? Because they would become more powerful."

Uh oh, Peter thought. This wasn't a time to hold back. He confessed immediately, "Um, Adell. Ah, Mig doesn't know this, but I brought him back."

Adell gaped at him. After a minute, she sighed. "Well, you are lucky he is a good man. Be careful not to make this mistake again."

When he returned from his walk with Adell, Peter told Mig and Carrie that he was ready to go if they were. "I am," said Mig.

Carrie nodded, "Yes, me too!"

Announcing their intentions to Adell, she handed Carrie a small folded paper. As Carrie took it, Adell said, "Peter tells me the tomatoes from my garden are the best he's ever had. Please take this small gift of tomato seeds with you, and remember us as you grow them. I'm only sorry to know food has changed so much in your time."

Carrie thanked her and gave her a hug. Mig hugged Adell too, then he, Carrie, and Peter walked down the valley the way they'd come.

"Did you find what you needed here?" Carrie asked.

"Yes." Peter sighed. "I believed Roman *is* the murderer we've been chasing. He's been running circles around us, but now I know what we have to do to stop him and save those women. You two need to know that because he is a time traveler, I'll have to kill him. Adell confirmed this."

When they'd walked a half-mile away from the compound, Peter stopped. "Concentrate on home. Mig, maybe it'll be good practice if you help me. You're for sure part of our time-traveling family now."

The three bowed their heads and concentrated, and with a puff were gone from the forest.

29 – It's Time

Carrie awoke. She felt Mig shifting on the bed. It was their own bed, and it felt especially cozy after the uncomfortable nights sleeping on the floor of Adell and Adam's odd house. She reached over and patted Mig. "Good morning, husband."

Mig rolled over to face her. "Good morning, wife," he said, and kissed her. "Ready for some twenty-first century coffee?"

Carrie laughed. "Now that sounds good to me." She flipped the blankets over him and climbed out of bed. "Oh, it is so nice to wake up on an actual mattress."

Carrie made coffee while Mig pulled clean mugs out of the dishwasher. As soon as the coffee was ready, they filled their mugs and headed for the couch, sharing another good-morning kiss along the way.

"We need to get some work done today," Mig said.

Carrie reminded him that they hadn't actually been away several days in the present time, but in fact had worked the day before.

"What day is it?" Mig asked.

Carrie consulted her cell phone. "This thing says it's Monday."

"That makes sense," Mig said, "we left on Sunday." He paused, then added, "Amazing how we could be gone so long and still come back overnight."

"It's crazy," Carrie said. She smiled, "I guess we're all crazy now, not just Peter."

Mig laughed.

Carrie looked at Mig. His eyes were bright, if a little tired around the edges. "We had better squeeze in some time for grocery shopping... and start Christmas shopping soon. Yeah, things are crazy, but we can't save the world and let down the kids."

"You're right about that," Mig said, rubbing his eyes.

Mig had started drinking his coffee when Peter phoned. "Roman is coming by my house tonight. This is the day I told him I'd time travel with him to see where his children were killed. He doesn't know we know he's lying and that there are no children he's trying to save. Are you two ready to help me get this done today?"

Mig said they were ready, and Peter asked them to come by at 3 P.M.

Ending the call, Mig hugged his wife. "It's almost show-time. How about we take a quick trip to the mall?"

Carrie shuddered, her face grim. "Yeah, please, distract me from what we're going to do tonight. It was one thing to plan to save those women, but now we're on a path to kill the killer? How can we even do that? Even if he's a really bad guy who can time travel and do more bad things, can we take part in causing his death, and then just carry on with our lives?"

Mig held her tight. "I don't want to do it. You don't want to do it. I don't think Peter wants to kill him, especially since he's related to him. But, according to Peter, Adell said it's the only way to save Silvia and the other women *and* have them stay safe. The whole trip back to 1898 was for him to find out if there was any other way. This is it."

She nestled her head against his shoulder. "What about the whole, thou shalt not kill thing?"

Mig sighed. He leaned back and put his hands on the sides of her face. "Sweetheart, I believe we're meant to do this, and we'll be forgiven. Our intentions are good."

He pulled her close again and they stayed in each other's arms for a while.

***

Carrie and Mig arrived at Peter's house promptly at 3 o'clock.

Peter reviewed the plan, which would start immediately on Roman's arrival at 10 P.M. It involved Mig using his abilities to hold Roman in the present, starting when he arrived. They would then travel with Roman back in time to the date of the first murder, where the plan was to kill past-Roman, which would also kill the present-Roman they'd transported with them. Carrie would help comfort his victim, Silvia Andrews.

As the three discussed the plan in Peter's office, with maps and papers spread across his desk, Peter's doorbell rang. Peter looked up the stairs, then back at the Weathers. "He's hours early. I hope we're prepared enough. You two please stay here." Not waiting for confirmation, Peter took the stairs up two at a time.

"What do we do? Do we hide?" Carrie whispered.

"No," Mig whispered back. "Just hold on a second."

They listened intently. Carrie heard a lilting voice speaking with Peter. "What do I do when you grab him?"

Mig shushed her gently, then stepped between her and the office doorway. "Stay back, for now."

They heard Peter's footsteps coming down the stairs with a second, slower set of footprints following. Carrie felt her heart pounding.

Peter reached the office doorway and motioned with his hand for Mig to "stay put" as Roman followed him into the office. Carrie's mouth went dry; the rest of her began to sweat. She watched as the old man shuffled into the room leaning on a cane for support. He looked frail, gaunt; nothing like the killer she'd envisioned. Then, she remembered the personas. It was all an act.

Roman stepped toward the desk, halting when he noticed Mig and Carrie. His expression turned angry, but was quickly replaced by a too-wide smile under dark eyes. *He's not as smooth as Peter is at covering his emotions*, Carrie thought.

Through the forced smile, Roman asked, "Are we all going to travel together today? Splendid. I must get to know you both if Peter is giving away our family secrets to you."

Peter swung around as if to introduce them. Instead, he grabbed Roman by his shirt, twisting him until his arm was around the old man's neck. Peter tightened his arm against Roman's throat. "You're a murderer, Roman, and we're stopping this cat-and-mouse game right now."

Mig stepped forward, grabbing one of Roman's flailing arms. "We'll keep him here. Carrie, get the chair."

Mig stepped to the side as Carrie approached, rolling one of the desk chairs ahead of her. Peter pushed Roman into the chair, keeping hold around his neck. "Mig, get him by both wrists."

Mig moved in front of Roman and grabbed both, evading a kick from the seated man.

Breathlessly, Roman croaked, "You can't. Let me go."

"No," Peter hissed into his ear. "You think I couldn't figure you out? You walk in here pretending you need help, and all the time you have blood on your hands? You're staying put, and we're going to deal with you right now."

Peter let go of Roman's neck but kept both hands on the older man's shoulders. Through gritted teeth, Peter said, "You took lives. For nothing. Each of those women... you played games with their fates, Roman."

Roman laugh. "You, you're a dabbler, Peter! You're like a squirrel gathering little bits of things while I own the forest. I have friends in high places all through time. I am the only one who can judge what I do. How foolish you are. You don't know half the possibilities open to us. You're incapable of understanding the power we have. What power *I* have. I eclipse you, and your muddled grandfather Alfonso! I'll kill you just for the fun of it."

"You're a monster." Peter gripped Roman's shoulders harder. Mig took a step forward, pushing Roman's wrists to his chest.

Roman laughed. "I took their lives. I gave them back their lives. Maybe I'll take them again. So, what harm? Fun is fun!" His laughter increased to a full-throated roar, his enjoyment so palpable Peter couldn't stand it.

"Enough!" Peter yelled, pushing down hard on Roman's shoulders. The old man winced.

Carrie knew the next part of the plan called for Roman to be rolled into the time travel room, to be forced back in time with Peter and Mig. She began moving, slowly inching her way toward the panel.

Roman spotted her and growled. "I'll kill you next, girlie," followed by a string of curses as Peter and Mig began rolling the chair.

As Roman swore, the memory flashed in Peter's mind of his pursuer falling down a hill near a pond months ago. Roman had gotten the drop on Peter that night. Unlike then, Peter now had the advantage.

His grip tightened on Roman's shoulders. "You're never going to hurt anyone again."

Roman laughed again. "Excuse me while I pop off. You're a mere time dabbler, Peter. You can't hold me here."

Peter held tightly, Mig firmly grasped Roman's wrists and pushing him backward toward the desk. "Mig, focus on him being *here*," Peter whispered. Mig nodded. Just as Peter had held Mig in place and time during their lessons, and just as they'd planned, the two men kept Roman from traveling.

Suddenly, Roman yelped. "What are you doing? You can't do this. I'm stronger than you--" his face swiveled up to stare at Mig. "How are you..." but he didn't finish his question.

It was Peter's turn to laugh. "Didn't expect it to be two travelers against one, did you?"

Carrie stepped up, watching as black flashes came and went, her heart pounding.

"Not just two," an unfamiliar voice said.

Mig jumped, holding fast to Roman's arm, and faced a new arrival in the room. "Where--"

Peter gasped. "Grampa!" but before he'd finished saying the word, his grandfather pushed a needle into Roman's arm and depressed the syringe. Roman drew in half a breath, growled, then groaned.

"He'll sleep now," Alfonso Horacio said. He pushed Peter and Mig aside and knelt in front of Roman, whose head had drooped to his chest, nodding as it rose and fell with his breathing. "Roman, old boy. Let go. Sleep, cousin. This is best for all, even you."

Carrie's anxiety rose, heartbeat increasing, and she felt the room spinning. The next thing she knew, Mig's arms were around her.

For a moment, she couldn't understand why she was sitting on the floor. Her eyes focused and she saw Peter embracing the white-haired stranger who'd appeared out of nowhere. "Hello, I am Alfonso," he said, nodding to Carrie, then Mig, "I'm sad we're meeting under these unpleasant circumstances."

"Hello," Carrie said, her voice sounded much calmer than she felt.

"Grampa," Peter said, hugging the old man again. Carrie thought she had never seen Peter looking so drained.

"Good to see you, P.H., and your partners in time," Alfonso said, eyes twinkling. Carrie had the sudden thought that time jokes ran in the family.

Mig helped Carrie stand, then extended his hand to Alfonso. He grabbed Mig's hand in both of his and shook it.

"I wish I could stay and be the fourth Musketeer," Alfonso said, "but I don't have strength enough to be your d'Artagnan for more than this short time."

Stepping close to Peter's side, he said, "I'm here to help you stop Roman, P.H. I thought I was early..."

"Roman came early." Peter's voice dropped to a whisper. "I'm so glad you came, Grampa. Thank you."

The newcomer shrugged. "Better my cousin's death is on my conscience than yours, my boy. Take me where you want him to be stopped."

Then, Alfonso spoke to Mig. "You hold Roman tightly as you were doing before. Hold him here. If the drug wears off, and he wakes up, you must not let him travel in time to escape." He walked quickly into the time travel room, Peter at his heels.

"Don't we need to take Roman with us?" Peter asked.

Alfonso shook his head. "No. We have a time traveler who can hold him here." He gestured toward Mig. "Death there will be death for Roman here."

"But the Weathers have to be inside this room--"

"Roman cannot be in this room." To Mig, he said, "When you see Roman's body leaving, get across the threshold with your wife."

He turned to Peter. "P.H., we must go and stop him in the past. *When* are we going?"

"First of September, shortly before 1 A.M. I know *where* so I'll take us," Peter said. "But we need Carrie--"

Before Peter could finish, his grandfather put his hand on Peter's back and yelled, "Go now."

Carrie and Mig watched as the sparking came and the two men disappeared. She moved close to Mig, not touching him. "He didn't take us. What do I do?"

Mig said, "Help me get Roman by the time travel room doorway. I have to hold Roman here, the old man said. Let's hope Peter and his Grampa can stop him back then, and fast."

"Are you sure? What if we aren't in the room on time?"

Mig paused for one heartbeat before answering, "I don't know, but it's the only plan we have at this point. They're gone. You and I have to be in that room, and I have to hold him, so let's just do it as best we can."

30 – Back to September

Peter and his grandfather Alfonso arrived in the first hour of the first of September, and stood watch. Peter had selected the destination and time, knowing it would mean Silvia Andrews was about to be murdered, and it was their best chance to stop Roman and to save her. Once she was saved, any women killed after her — at least, any whom Roman hadn't "corrected" away already — would also be saved. From what Carrie had found in the original victims' initials, the message SAVE THEM, Peter was confident that there were no serial victims before Silvia.

Peter said a short prayer that Mig and Carrie would make it into his secret room in time. If they were inside the room, they would retain their memories, both smoky and corrected.

A vehicle approached with no headlights. Peter could see his Grampa holding a finger to his lips, shushing him, although he'd been barely visible in the darkness.

They'd heard the car door open, followed by the sound of a woman crying — Silvia Andrews — and the deep, cursing voice Peter now knew well.

As his Grampa had moved left toward the noises, Peter moved right. His grandfather had insisted on taking on the task of killing Roman. So Peter wouldn't.

As Peter moved forward in the dark, he fell into the pattern he and his Grampa had always had working together. Retirement or not, Peter knew Grampa could do it.

Peter had found the help he needed after all, but not in the way he'd imagined. He knew Mig was holding Roman in place, preventing his escape. As he and his Grampa closed in on the murderer and his victim in the dark, Peter no longer feared this was too much for Grampa, that he might lose him. He'd been underestimating Alfonso.

The sobbing had moved so close that he could hear sniffling, too. Flashes of light came and went. It looked to Peter like Roman had a flashlight in his hand.

At that point, he knew Grampa was somewhere on the opposite side of Roman. Peter couldn't see him, but he knew he was in place.

As Roman pushed the crying woman to the ground, the flashlight illuminated, giving Peter Roman's exact position.

His grandfather moved as Peter did, both closing in quickly and silently. Then had come more cursing. As Alfonso's arm circled Roman's neck, the flashlight swung upward, almost catching Peter in the head. Peter struck out with his forearm, and the flashlight fell to the ground and went out.

He felt his grandfather pushing downward on Roman and joined him in forcing the still-cursing man to the ground, landing hard on his rump with his legs sprawled in front of him. Alfonso was pulled down and shifted onto his knees behind Roman's back. Peter held Roman's arms firmly as Alfonso squeezed his forearm against Roman's neck, using his second arm to pull it tighter.

Off to the side, Peter heard the woman moving. She ran away, thankfully in the direction of the road. The sound of his grandfather's breathing, and Roman's gurgling, were joined by the sound of bare feet running. Peter heard her stumble several times before the sobbing dissipated and her footsteps change to the slapping of feet-on-asphalt as she reached the road and ran up it. He held Roman's arms, avoiding kicks from his legs, as Alfonso squeezed.

Alfonso let out a snarl as he leaned backward, using his weight to choke Roman harder, ensuring he wasn't passed out, but dead.

Then, there was silence, save for the harsh sound of his grandfather's breathing. Roman was gone. Alfonso released his grasp and the body dropped to the ground.

A moment later, Alfonso panted, "It's done. It had to be done."

Mig held onto Roman as Carrie pushed the chair toward the time travel room's threshold.

As they reached it, the chair thumped against the bookshelf. Roman thrashed once, his leg rising and catching Carrie in the stomach. With an "oof," she lost her balance and fell, hitting her head against Peter's desk.

Mig let go to run to his wife, then realized he couldn't and immediately returned his hands to Roman's shoulders. "Are you all right, Carrie?"

Blood flowed from the cut on her head, drawing a red path across her cheek. "I'm coming," she said, her voice strained.

"You're bleeding! Get into the room. Hurry!"

Carrie crawled on all fours, squeezing past the chair containing Roman and past Mig's legs into the secret room. "You have to be with me."

"It'll be okay," Mig said, his voice rising. "I'll be there." He gripped Roman hard, glancing over his shoulder to confirm Carrie was fully inside. She sat in the center of the small room, blood running down her face and onto her shirt. "Press something on it. I'll be there in a second."

Mig pulled at the chair. Almost to the threshold, he saw Roman's legs begin to spark. Mig let go of the chair and stepped backward over the threshold and into the time travel room.

He watched as the sparkling darkness ate Roman away to nothing, leaving the chair empty.

Stunned for a moment, Mig realized that the air didn't smell the way it did when he time traveled with Peter. The scent of rotten fruit increased, and he understood. Roman had gone away like the rook, disappearing forever.

Leaving the panel open, he hurried to Carrie. "Okay," he said after checking her wound, "it's small. Head wounds just bleed like crazy. You'll be okay."

He held her as the now familiar, calming baby scent overwhelmed them.

They slept.

Peter picked up the flashlight, and he and Alfonso staged the scene. In the dark, he was sure Silvia Andrews couldn't have seen them. Even if she had heard the scuffle, Peter hoped she'd be more focused on her survival than on trying to recount details of noises she heard in the dark while terrified for her life. If they made it look like an accident, she likely wouldn't say otherwise.

Peter stared at Roman's body. "Adell told me he won't go to his nest unless he was time traveling to here."

Alfonso took several heavy breaths, then said, "She's right. We've killed him while we were traveling, but apparently he was not. This past-Roman is in its own time, and so the police will find him here where he has fallen. The Roman we left with Mig, well, he'll disappear."

Poof, Peter thought. "Mig will understand. I've shown him the difference between traveling and how things out of time are taken away. I hope he had time to get into the room with Carrie."

As Alfonso wiped at Roman's neck and clothing to remove any of their fingerprints, Peter used the light to find a tree branch on the ground. They pulled his body toward it, then placed the heavy branch across Roman's neck, repositioning past-Roman's body on the ground. It wasn't a good staging, but it was, Peter thought, good enough that the police could call it an accident. Especially since they would have a living victim to tell them what Roman had done to her before his "accident" and her escape.

Peter let out a sigh of relief. In the distance, he heard a siren and looked at his Grampa.

Peter gave his Grampa a long hug. When he finally released him, the old man tousled his hair. Wearily, he said, "Good-bye, P.H."

A moment later, Alfonso headed to his adopted place in the future, and Peter returned to his own time.

Carrie blinked awake and stared at the ceiling. She felt Mig stir next to her. Suddenly, he bolted upright. He scooped Carrie into his arms. "How does your head feel? Are you okay?"

She rubbed his cheek and smiled. "I am." He hugged her tight, and she kissed him on the cheek. "I do love you," she whispered.

Mig kissed the top of her head where it was not injured, from which blood had flowed and terrified him. He'd kept pressure on her wound, even as she'd drifted off, crusting blood across her face. What mattered now was that the correction had been made. She was all right. "I was afraid you'd stay hurt since you were bleeding inside Peter's little room."

She looked into his eyes. "Me too."

Clearing his throat, Mig said, "Peter will be home. We need to call the man."

Peter awoke with a mix of emotions. He lay on his bed a long time, thinking, before reluctantly climbing out of bed. He padded to the bathroom, showered, dressed quickly, and headed for his office.

He missed his grandfather even more for the brief encounter; the old wound caused by Alfonso's departure had reopened. Peter was relieved to have seen him, to know he was doing all right.

He was more relieved to have finally accomplished his goal — with many helping hands — of stopping the time-traveler-serial-killer. From the changes he felt on the timeline, he knew the Weathers had both made it into the time travel room. He'd check on them soon.

First, Peter checked online, and was relieved to read an old news story from September about the woman, her escape, and reaching help at a house down the road. This first article he'd found was an early one and her name hadn't been given, but Peter knew it: Silvia Andrews. Her name was confirmed in later news articles from September.

Mention was made in several articles regarding an unknown man, found dead in a wooded area nearby, believed to be her attacker. The word "accident" was used in articles written by several newspapers and TV news sites, and Peter relaxed significantly. A consensus had been reached, and he was free of suspicion, along with his grandfather.

There was no mention of other witnesses or of Samaritans helping Silvia to escape, and Peter wondered exactly what — if anything — Silvia might have heard. He'd never contact her to find out. His work was done.

He was just picking up his cell phone to call Mig, when his phone rang. Seeing it was Mig calling, he grinned and pressed the button to answer. "Hello, Mig. What's up?"

31 – Better Days

Before she knew it, Carrie had acclimated to her and Mig's new life as time travelers. They fell into a routine. Saturday classes became weekly meals with Peter. They three planned corrections together, and Mig became expert at moving the three of them through time, to Peter's glee.

There were tumultuous moments. The Saturday when Peter sat them down and recounted a very long tale from his travels — one that began with, "I've known you both well as Mig has suspected" — and ended with Mig and Carrie horrified to learn of their own deaths and Peter's corrections to reunite them. It took Carrie longer to get over than it did Mig, but eventually they were back at it, the three planning and traveling.

Carrie became less afraid after she learned she had, in fact, worked with Peter before, and had survived widowhood.

They had both surprised Peter by trusting him more afterward, not less. The Weathers folded him into their family — even having him take part in the conversation when they told their children of Mig's unique family line.

The first of April, Carrie presented Peter with a tray of tomato seedlings as they walked in his front door. "From Adell's seeds," she said. He thanked her, taking the tray and carrying it into his kitchen.

As soon as they were seated, Peter announced, "Mig, Carrie, I think you're ready to travel without me. Or, rather, I'll stay in the time travel room instead of going with you. My request for your first trip on your own is that you go to 2006 and be so kind as to stop by my house and introduce yourselves to my grandfather."

Carrie clasp her hands, murmuring, "On our own. Wow."

Mig answered, "Sounds like a good plan to me."

Peter had chosen a date when he knew past-him had been, would be, away from the house while his Grampa would be there. "I just want you to meet him, and him to meet the two of you. He's an important man in my eyes, and I'd like him to know I'm passing on what he taught me. But, remind him not to tell the me-back-then of your visit. Of course, don't tell my grandfather about how *he* stopped Roman, either."

Carrie thought she saw Peter's eyes glaze but a moment later they cleared. Peter added, "Plus, if you two have trouble getting home, my Grampa can help you to return safely."

Mig extended his hand and Peter shook it. "Thank you for letting us be a part of this, Peter. We hope to make you proud."

Peter grasped Mig's hand with both of his. "Once you have this solo trip under your belt, let's plan for you and Carrie to go and meet your grandparents."

"Absolutely. And since we're family, you should come with us, Peter. Cousin."

"Wonderful. Now, you two should go." He led them into the time travel room and he and Mig sorted out the location, time, and date.

"Have a nice trip and I'll talk with you tomorrow."

That evening, as Peter struggled to adjust the pillow and blankets on the floor of his time travel room, Mig and Carrie arrived on Peter's patio back on a warm Spring morning in 2006.

Peter's grandfather emerged from the house a moment later. "Hello," he said pleasantly, though Carrie saw puzzlement in his eyes. "Nice of you to pop in for a visit. Now tell me: *Who are you?*"

Mig held up his hand and waved. "I'm Mig, and this is my wife Carrie. We're friends of Peter's."

"Good to meet friends of my grandson. Please, come in," he said, leading them into the room they knew as Peter's office. It surprised Carrie that the office looked the same as in their time, with one exception: Peter's disheveled papers were missing from the desk and bookshelves.

Alfonso easily accepted that his visitors were from the future. He was more jovial and socially adept than his grandson, Carrie observed.

After a time, Alfonso stood, then recommended they return to their time and give Peter his regards.

Mig explained that Peter needed Alfonso not to mention to then-Peter that they had visited. Since Mig and Carrie were not yet in his lives, Peter thought it best for then-Peter to not learn he would be training them as time travelers in his future. Alfonso agreed. "Smart boy, that grandson of mine."

He led them to his back patio. "Since it sounds like you two are new to time traveling, I think perhaps it will be easier for you to go back to your time from this location."

Mig laughed, "Peter said the same thing."

"I'm pleased he has remembered my teachings," Alfonso said, smiling. He excused himself, shut the patio door, and left them.

Mig and Carrie briefly discussed taking a walk around downtown before leaving. Then, Mig pointed out they might bump into themselves or their children. "And back then we had no idea this was possible. If one of the kids sees us and talks to us, then mentions it to ourselves from now, we'll never be able to understand what's going on. Let's just head back to our own time."

Carrie gripped his hands, kissed him, and they both closed their eyes, Mig concentrating, on home. When the *poof* happened, Carrie felt overwhelming joy at what they'd done. They had traveled back, on Mig's ability, and were now going forward again. They were really time travelers. *Well, Mig is. I'm a sidekick.*

She awoke the next morning, reached her arm over Mig, and squeezed. "Good morning, fellow time traveler."

Mig laughed, then turned to face her. He put his arm around her, gave her a long kiss, and said, "Good morning, wife."

They stayed in bed longer than normal, reviewing their trip back to meet Peter's Grampa, their return trip, and waking up safe-and-sound in their bed. That they'd successfully time traveled astounded them both.

Eventually, they got out of bed. Mig made coffee while Carrie washed their coffee mugs. Then, Mig called Peter while the coffee brewed.

Peter answered the phone with, "Welcome back!"

"Thank you," Mig said. "You remember?"

"Of course," Peter laughed. "You didn't wipe out my yesterday or anything. Good job!"

Mig laughed too, "That was cool as heck! And your Grampa, he's a really nice guy."

"Yes, he is," Peter replied. "I'm glad you three had a chance to talk. Your first meeting was...unpleasant. My Grampa never told me you'd visited him, so that's good. No confusion or derailing of things. You enjoy the rest of the day, Mig, and perhaps you and Carrie can come by and see me this weekend. Perhaps, Saturday morning around 10 A.M.?"

"Sure, be happy to. See you Saturday morning. Good-bye," Mig said, then ended the call.

Over their coffee, Mig and Carrie traded notes about the trip and their new memories of meeting Alfonso. Since they

hadn't changed anything except what Peter's grandfather knew
— and he hadn't told Peter of their visit — there wasn't much in
the way of foggy memories.

32 – Family Moments

One beautiful Saturday in May, just after their youngest's college classes ended for the semester, Peter was off on a regular ol' plane trip to New Mexico for a visit and to start his long-planned research on canines and their possible retention of smoky memories. Mig had emailed Peter that morning, teasingly implying Peter was there for Angie Bly, not her dog.

With no obligations, Mig and Carrie drove to Topsail Island to enjoy beach time with the kids and grandchildren, including a new one on the way.

Comfortably sprawled on a towel with long stretches of beach in both directions, Carrie breathed in the salt air contentedly. Down the strand, she watched Mig tossing a football with Dylan and Junior. *Three generations playing ball*, she thought, then noted Mig's hair was a little darker, his skin smoother, than their beach day at the end of the previous summer.

Dylan's wife was in a beach chair near Carrie, her extended belly drawing a stream of women from other parts of the beach, each of them asking, "How far along are you?" before asking if they could touch her belly. Brianna declined, letting out a long sigh as each new woman approached to ask the question.

Carrie saw Brianna's distress and moved slightly in front of her, to intercept any approaching, belly-wanna-touching strangers.

She heard Mig laughing in the distance, drawing her attention back to him and the boys. The boys ran for the ball Mig had thrown, with Dylan diving to catch it, spraying sand into the air as he puffed onto the beach. He rose, elatedly holding the ball up to show Mig he'd caught it, then tossed it to Junior. The three then re-joined Carrie and the rest of the family on their patch of beach.

Carrie handed Mig a beach towel as he approached. Mig shook the towel and spread it on the sand next to Carrie's, then sat down. He blew out a breath and raised his eyebrows in an exaggerated the-kids-wore-me-out face.

Carrie reached over and brushed a patch of sand from his shoulder. The two sat together, watching their grown kids and grandchildren. She saw Mig glance toward Brianna, and knew he was thinking of the new grandchild to come.

Confirming her thought, Mig said, "I can't wait to bring that baby to the beach and dip its tiny toes into the ocean for the first time." He brushed sand off of his towel. The wind blew, and sand covered everyone and everything. He brushed at the towel again, as Carrie gently dusted her face with her t-shirt.

Mig turned toward Carrie. In a low voice, he asked, "So, what do you think Peter is really doing in New Mexico?"

She laughed. "Next time we'll have to bring him with us so we can keep tabs on him. He is family, after all."

Epilogue

The dog ran down the mountain, and Peter followed slowly. He enjoyed the mountain air and was in no hurry. Max wouldn't go far, he knew. The dog was protective and never strayed more than a minute from Peter's side when he walked her for Angie.

Peter reached the valley floor where Max was waiting. Checking the map in his hands, he looked around until he found the trail he wanted. With a hundred-plus years of forest growth, there was no way he could recognize the place they'd been back in 1898. According to the map, if he continued for a half-mile more, he'd be where the family compound had been.

He wondered if any of it would still be standing. Over 100 years had passed since he'd visited with the Weathers, met Adell, and held his newborn grandfather.

As he reached the bottom of valley floor, he spotted a shimmer in the distance. The trees surrounding the odd house were taller, but its shape was solid.

Sweating now, Peter followed Max up the valley toward the compound. Stopping to wipe his brow, Max slowed and stepped in front of Peter, facing toward their destination. Looking ahead, Peter saw a familiar face, hand shielding her eyes from the sun, watching them.

"It's okay, Max," he said, walking forward. He waved as he and Max approached.

Adell waved back.

About The Author

K. F. Whatley's professional writing experience spans twenty years. Starting her journey authoring nonfiction desktop publishing books, then moving into news reporting in 2011, Whatley dove into fiction in 2006 — picking up where her teen self had left off.

After publishing short items in local literary journals, she made the leap with publication of her first novel in 2018. *Making Corrections*, the first novel in the Weathers-Braggin time travel series, was re-released in 2020 in-advance of *Triad of Time*.

Based in Eastern North Carolina, with ocean in one direction and foothills in the other, she fills her time with writing for work and pleasure, family gatherings, gardening, and trying not to trip over house cats.